Why Not Them?

Why Not Them? How One Man's Love for His Son Born with Down Syndrome Is Changing the World for Persons with Disabilities

by Lloyd M. Lewis, as told to Corinne Joy Brown, ©2018.

ISBN: 978-1-947841-60-4

With thanks to Erica Porter, Michelle Sie Whitten, Dominick Rivera and Corinne Brown for most of the images and Stevie Crecilius of Wonderworks Studios for the back cover shot.

Book design by AE Books, Denver, CO.

First Printing by Steuben Press. Longmont, CO. 80501

Praise for Why Not Them

"Very, very well written, heartfelt, compelling, and moving ... quite a piece from the heart!"

—Craig Fleishman, founder of Jason Fleishman Camp
for Children with Epilepsy

"Thanks for giving me the opportunity to read this important book. To see the work Lewis has done is not only inspiring to read about, but spiritually uplifting to realize its impact on individuals and upon society."

—Rabbi Raymond Zwerin, Temple Sinai, Denver CO

"Lloyd combines years of experience both as a practitioner and as a parent to provide unique perspective and best practices on how we can better serve the families of children with Down syndrome and other intellectual disabilities."

—Jamie Van Leeuwen, Global Livingston Institute

Why Not Them?

How One Man's Love for His Son Born with Down Syndrome
Is Changing the World for Persons with Disabilities

by Lloyd M. Lewis

as told to Corinne Joy Brown

To Kennedy, and to Claire, Hannah and Aidan, and all of our wonderful arc Ambassadors ...

Contents

Prologue

I walked the hallway and paced the floor like any expectant father, looking alternately at my watch and the clock staring back at me on the wall. It was close to seven o'clock. My partner had gone into labor earlier than we expected. Although I had rushed over to join her as fast as I could, I was more than an hour from the hospital, and she was already well under way when I arrived. As I sped toward her, anxious and excited, I kept thinking that no matter who you are, nothing equals the anticipation and concern over the birth of a child—after all, a new human being was coming into the world.

At the time, in the fall of 2003, I was 48 years old and quite far along in raising a family. I had teenagers already, a boy and two girls, and had to brace myself to think that I'd be adding another little one soon. We'd learned earlier from the ultrasound that our baby was a boy, and decided we would call him Kennedy. The name we arrived at happened to be the name of one of my childhood heroes, a man who had made a difference and left an enduring legacy. That much I knew. The obstetrician had also suggested an amniocentesis midway through the pregnancy, but we passed on that idea, thinking it wasn't important. I'm not really sure what I would have advocated then, though I know now, it would not have made a difference.

When the delivery doctor came through the door into the waiting room, I could tell immediately by his demeanor that something was wrong.

"I'm afraid I don't have very good news," the doctor said, his face unusually grave.

"What is it?" I asked, not sure I wanted to know.

"We suspect Down syndrome," he answered in his most professional tone. "I'm so very sorry." A proclamation of doom.

"What do you mean you're sorry?" I asked, more curious than surprised, a ripple of concern furrowing my brow. Unfamiliar with the term, I asked, "Down syndrome?" I'd heard of it, but that was all. "What does it mean?"

"It's something like Mongolism," he said. "As in—not normal. If I'm correct, you and your wife have a very rough road ahead."

I was stunned by his answer and, temporarily, unable to respond. I shook my head, filled with disbelief. No, I thought, he had to be mistaken. He couldn't be talking about our baby.

Not in my world. No way. I contemplated his remark silently, facing him, and stared into his eyes. What did it really mean?

As I waited for more information, a feeling like an electric shock rippled through me, confirming that my life was going to change. Nothing would ever be the same. At the time, I was working as a CFO for a high-tech company. I never dreamed that our family life could shift in an instant, or that anything irreparable could come my way. I was shaken by the doctor's negative prognosis and ushered him out of the room, asking adamantly that he not return. His use of the outdated and damning term "Mongolism," something I *had* heard of, offended me to the core.

*****

Around us, hospital nurses moved with deliberation, skirting the bed in respectful silence. No one said a word. Gone was the usual atmosphere of joy and triumph after a new baby is born. It felt like we were in a morgue. After some of the nurses and another doctor reviewed the assessment and explained the situation further, we tried to be accepting, still not fully appreciating what the language implied. The term "Down syndrome" sounded so foreign. We needed more.

"Can I see him please?" I asked, determined not to be frightened by what I didn't understand.

Kennedy had been moved to the infant nursery for further tests and much-needed oxygen. I begged the nurses to let me hold him in my arms and reassure myself that everything was going to be okay. At the same time, I promised our little newborn that, unlike some parents who might have been set back by this kind of news, we would stay the course; we would never abandon him, no matter what, and that, whatever it took, we'd both be there.

What I needed to learn was just what kind of life awaited this innocent child, and then, determine my role, whatever it was going to be. The challenge loomed bigger than anything I had ever faced before. I also needed to reassure his mother and myself that we could handle it, one way or another. Little did I know that an immeasurable opportunity lay before me—an opportunity and a blessing.

With an overwhelming feeling of both humility and gratitude from that moment on, I set out to explore the mystery of how the birth of our son would change the way I lived, the way I saw the world, and what really mattered. Kennedy's survival, growth, and development allowed me to take his disability, Down syndrome, and appreciate the miracle of his birth. This journey also led me to tackle the complete reorganization and repurposing of a large, nonprofit organization that today exclusively serves many hundreds of others with intellectual and developmental disabilities across greater Colorado.

My ongoing commitment to my child and to all those individuals—including their complete fulfillment as human beings—and to this vast field of study and research has deepened over the years and continues to do so every single day. Kennedy's arrival has helped open the doors for thousands, bringing them joy and self-respect, and changed the way they live. In fact, the way the rest of us live, too.

Lloyd M. Lewis

More importantly, by acknowledging Kennedy's disability and accepting it, the world I inhabit can now view the birth of a child with disabilities as an event to be celebrated as much as any other. The traditional feelings of pity and sadness experienced by parents, once so common, must instead be replaced with understanding. Persons with disabilities, I am so very proud to say, have much to give and teach us all.

Best of all, I realize as I write these words, that the story I want to tell isn't over. In fact, it's really just begun, especially because I have seen the effect one person can have by leading with compassion. It's a lesson I've learned, and it's simple. First, you have to fill your heart with love, and then, share it with everyone you know.

Chapter One

Meet arc Thrift
A Modern-Day Miracle

"Some people dream of success; others make it happen."

—Unknown

In a utopian world, no one is ever left behind, each person has the same chances as the next, and we all have the same possibilities for success. That's the promise—the "American dream." But as I have learned in my own life, the real world has its own ideas. Things don't always go as planned. Some of us face greater challenges than others, and some of us need individual help and support. Some of us have to work much harder than the rest, every single day of our lives.

In greater metro Denver, a unique business thrives in response to this imperfect world; a tax-exempt, nonprofit company called arc Thrift Stores that offers secondhand merchandise at enticingly affordable prices. Like millions of other businesses, it's retail; one small part of a huge sector of America's GNP; the flow of goods for cash, simple supply and demand, something every businessman understands. At the end of each year, companies big and small that deal in sales look forward to calculating the gross margin or profit. But at the cash registers of arc Thrift, that's only half the story.

1

At the end of arc Thrift's year, our most treasured benefit is calculated in increased human self-worth and self-esteem, a byproduct of providing a livelihood for hundreds of employees who were born with intellectual and developmental disabilities. At arc Thrift Stores, a thriving business has been built on uplifting a unique sector of humanity, and our monetary profits support the advocacy, employment, well-being, and inclusion of valuable men and women who might have never been given a chance to be independent and fulfilled. Our company is dedicated to creating and funding programs that serve those individuals living with intellectual and developmental disabilities, and who have complex and evolving needs. At our core, our company believes that all people in this community should have the opportunity to decide how they live, learn, work, and play.

*****

Creating a new paradigm for employing persons with disabilities doesn't happen overnight. It takes the work of hundreds of employees and hundreds of volunteers, as well. It takes big thinking, imagination, and an appetite for risk. It takes courage and requires patience, compassion, and the ability to see past the idealized version of what men and woman should look, think, and be like.

Most of all, it takes guts to persevere in the face of disbelievers. For me, it took a vision formed more than a decade ago that continues to refocus with each new dawn. I should know. I've been there every step of the way, and I am still dreaming of ever-more perfect versions of this amazing dream. The story I'm about to tell you aims to help you understand how that vision became all I could see on my immediate and far distant horizons, exactly how the vision changed me, and how it might change you, too. It might be a springboard for something extraodinary and far-reaching in your own life, for the greater good, and for your own self-worth. I'm hoping that it will.

> Hiring people with disabilities is a plus, not a minus. There's room for them in every single business. They make the perfect employees.

Chapter Two

Fulfilling the Dream

"The essence of being human is that one does not seek perfection."

—*George Orwell, novelist*

The great state of Colorado prides itself on its diversity. This is a place rich in varied demographics, where people from every background are welcome to settle and make their home, and who do so in continuing droves. By and large, its citizens are open, engaging, and accepting. It's part of why I love living here.

Until recently, however, one population was largely underserved—individuals with developmental disabilities. Looking as far back as the 1950s, more than 90 percent of such individuals who lived in Colorado, as well as in other states nationwide, had no source of gainful employment. Most of them, following high school, simply remained at home with their families into adulthood.

The situation remained the same here for decades—until the 1960s, when the idea of employing individuals with disabilities was first encouraged. Until our stores and others began to implement this unique work philosophy in earnest, however, many thought it impractical or impossible to employ persons with intellectual or physical disabilities at all, on either a large or small scale. Few precedents existed at the time; there was very little to build on. Many naysayers said it couldn't be done. But we at arc Thrift Stores are proving them wrong.

All our arc Thrift–funded programs, stores, and educational opportunities were, at their conception, more than just ideas; they became a viable mission and a goal, as well as the heart of a veritable community. The full realization of that goal didn't happen overnight, and it wasn't easy; but by following the dream of a better world by promoting inclusion of those with special needs, arc Thrift Stores created a work model that promotes individually tailored employment opportunities for adults with intellectual and physical disabilities all across Colorado's Front Range. And not just for a few individuals, but for hundreds!

Sounds challenging, doesn't it?

Well, here's the good news; the challenge has been met. We did what couldn't be done. Those once cast aside by so many have unimagined new opportunities.

*****

Long before I came into the picture in 2005, Arc of the United States chapters in Colorado were already established across the state. The idea for arc Thrift Stores, the chain of retail stores in Colorado that offered inclusivity and support, was preceded by the founding of this parent organization, back in the 1940s.

Arc of the United States was one of the first organizations founded by parents of children with intellectual and developmental disabilities. Initially, it was created to petition for humane treatment of those who were housed in large institutions, followed by advocacy for deinstitutionalization, mainstreaming, and inclusion in society—a worthy and important mission. It arose at a time when ideas about how to care for and treat those with disabilities were finally changing; these ideas were long overdue, precipitating a new era of care and medical research. But it was a young organization, just finding its way, and a great deal of science, intervention, advocacy, and a much-needed shift in public perception and understanding were yet to follow.

Today, hundreds of local Arc chapters exist across the United States. They make up one of the country's ten largest nonprofit organizations. Colorado boasts fourteen of these advocacy chapters located from as far south of Denver as Pueblo, to Fort Collins in the north, and across the Western Slope. These chapters are comprised of families and advocates who work with thousands of individuals with intellectual and development disabilities, helping them to find jobs, housing, medical services, assistance in schools, and varied social activities.

The company I head, "arc Thrift Stores," is centered in metro Denver, and provides the majority of the funding to the Colorado chapters totaling nearly $70 million collected since 2005. We have made it more than possible for Arc to advocate for those in need. Our basic goal has been to create a profit so we can invest monies back into the these chapters, thereby offering various constructive programs supporting those with developmental disabilities.

How we do this is the real challenge. We manage to make this huge financial commitment thanks to our more than 27 arc Thrift retail stores and warehouses. (Soon to be 28.) We also host a program we call "Working for a Purpose," conducted throughout all the store locations, that helps to provide solid employment opportunities for all kinds of employees, including those who might otherwise find it difficult to obtain jobs.

Sounds amazing, doesn't it?

It is. It's a far-reaching, idealistic, and remarkable goal that we reset every single day, destined to be as riveting and exacting in the future as it was when we started. The inspiring program, Working for a Purpose, recruits, hires, trains, and mentors individuals who are born with challenges such as autism, Down syndrome, cerebral palsy, and other intellectual disabilities. It might sound improbable, but it's true—we hire employees with all of the above and more; individuals whom most people think are simply incapable of holding a job.

As founders of Working for a Purpose, we recognize that absolutely everyone can contribute to the world in some meaningful way. In keeping with that belief, we honor contributions large and small made by every one of the dedicated participants in our employ. Working for a Purpose also provides holistic, strength-based, supportive employment services along with practical, life-skills education and overall socialization opportunities.

Seem complex? It's not. In short, we engage and care for the whole person and try to make it fun. To that end, each month arc Thrift Stores, the company, offers a relaxing social outing, such as sharing a meal, participating in a physical activity such as bowling or sailing, or attending educational and entertaining events like a film or a trip to the zoo.

Make no mistake—the program Working for a Purpose is not a sheltered workshop. Rather, our enrollees are included in all aspects of legitimate work right alongside their more able-bodied peers! They are paid an hourly wage as well, slightly above minimum wage. This distinction says it all: Mainstreaming workers with disabilities leads to more self-sufficiency, self-confidence, and socialization, not to mention providing for a very stimulating workday for all concerned.

And guess what?

In return, hiring employees with disabilities has resulted in a lower turnover rate, better attendance and, initially, a doubling of company revenue. *Yes, doubling.* At this juncture, we can even say tripling. It's a formula for success that works. It's just good business and it creates a happy work place.

Have I got your attention yet? Good.

But wait—there's more.

Today, the formerly invisible population of persons with disabilities is becoming more visible, to their benefit and the benefit of society as a whole. It's time to see them for who they really are.

Chapter Three

The Back Story

"The road to glory begins with one step."

—Unknown

It's important to understand how my company got where we are today, considering that the newly formed chapters of Arc in Colorado relied solely on grassroots efforts. During the very humble beginnings, they held small fundraisers such as garage sales and bake sales to raise money to support their programs. Then, in 1963, the local chapters banded together and created Metropolitan Arc as a separate fundraising entity and nonprofit organization. They knew they needed to grow if they were going to survive, and their sole purpose was to raise funds for their many needs.

Back then, a board member from the Arc chapter in Front Range Jefferson, Clear Creek, and Gilpin counties near Denver attended a training session in California. While there, he visited and toured a thrift store operation. Intrigued, he brought the idea back to his metropolitan Arc colleagues. Could it be replicated here he wondered, hiring those with disabilities to work in such an environment?

In June of 1968, the first arc Thrift Store opened on South Broadway in Denver, the flagship location still operating today. When I came on board much later on, I saw the opportunity to run our stores more successfully with new ideas and a spirit of innovation. I believed we could expand even more rapidly than originally projected.

For the last decade, expansion under my lead has been exponential. Highly visible retail thrift stores across Denver are now supported by conveniently located neighborhood drop-off points. The arc Thrift logo with its charming bluebird can be seen throughout the city. In fact, at a time when more and more people are buying online, we have bucked the trend and are proving immediate satisfaction with brick-and-mortar locations filled with product. Buying secondhand no longer has any stigma—after all, everything vintage is in vogue. Buyers flock to the book and music departments as well as housewares and, of course, to seasonal decor and clothing. But we hear it time and time again—the human contact is as valuable as the bargain. People enjoy shopping in our stores.

Yes, I'm proud to say that practically no part of metropolitan Denver and most of Colorado is without arc Thrift Stores' presence today. Thanks to the continued dedication of our staff, and outstanding results measured in financial growth, human resources, and glowing smiles, we've done what no one thought possible —provided jobs for more than 300 individuals with disabilities in our overall workforce of 1,700 employees. Most of these workers are without college degrees (some without high school degrees) or technical training. We also employ numerous non-English speaking employees, and some who come from troubled backgrounds, including substance abuse and criminal histories. Some have been homeless, some are refugees. To us, they're all equal.

Sound like a miracle? I like to think of it that way, and so do many others.

I can tell you this: It's not just a dream or a business plan anymore. Our arc Thrift Stores have become a life-altering, game-changing, mind-blowing reality. We've learned that hiring people with disabilities is a major plus, not a minus. Each and every team member at every employment level is totally committed to making a difference, helping others, and working with those in need. We succeed because we have to, and because our people truly care about each other. More important, over the years since I've been the company's CEO, I've come to believe unequivocally that there must be room for employees with intellectual disabilities in every single business in Colorado, in the United States of America, on the planet, at all times, everyday, everywhere. I also believe that, in so many ways, persons with disabilities make the absolute perfect employees.

And I cannot wait to tell you why.

> Thanks to the birth of my son Kennedy, I became a passionate advocate for inclusion and acceptance of people with DS and other disabilities. If I can do it, so can the next person.

Chapter Four

When the Universe Intercedes

"I ask not for a lighter burden, but for broader shoulders."

—*Jewish proverb*

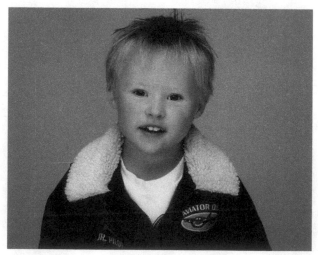

Kennedy Lewis

Following baby Kennedy's birth and the news that he had Down syndrome, my partner and I were presented with a situation neither of us really understood. The possibility of a child with any kind of intellectual disability had never come up, never even passed through our minds. We listened with intent as a maternity nurse quietly explained that raising our child, one out of 6,000 babies born with Down syndrome (DS) in America every year, would become our greatest challenge.

Just why did our son come into the world this way, we wondered. The truth is, we'll never know. It's nothing we did, or could have done. We were reassured that it was unrelated to our age (Kennedy's mother was in her early thirties), or the lifestyle we led, or any other external or internal factor. But when a birth like this happens, you stand frozen in place, overwhelmed by doubt. You feel isolated and alone. What could you have done differently? More importantly, how can you be the parent you need to be now? What skills will it take?

Kennedy's birth as a child with DS was indeed not the way things were planned—not quite the way we thought it would be. Although this little boy wasn't my first child, he was my partner's firstborn. And in the days that followed, we grew acutely more alone with our thoughts. We both realized we weren't just new parents; we were now also caretakers, and strangers to the particular requirements of our infant boy. We had work to do to close the gap. As mentioned, we were raising other children at the time, and we had no idea how the situation would impact our larger family.

As our new lives developed, Kennedy's mom would maintain home care and schedule appointments with therapists and doctors while I sought all the resources and education available on the outside. That's one of the main things I always did best: solve problems, find solutions, and take charge. As per usual, I was ready to give it my all.

Few can understand how overwhelming life seems when a child is born with a disability. I immersed myself in the search for guidance and information, unsure at the beginning where to turn. After all, I was used to making things right, keeping things under control, knowing it all. I was the one with the answers for everything, and always had been. At this juncture, I wanted solutions and direction in a hurry—I needed help.

*****

I started to investigate and read everything I could find out about Down syndrome. A genetic condition that cannot be "treated," DS is instead a challenge to be addressed at every phase of life. One in 800 persons is born with the condition; each person is different and unique. Down syndrome, also known as Trisomy 21, is caused by the presence of all (or part of) a third copy of chromosome 21. It's typically associated with physical growth delays, characteristic facial features, and mild to moderate intellectual disability.

The condition was named after John Langdon Down, the British doctor who fully described the syndrome in 1866. The genetic cause of Down syndrome—an extra copy of chromosome 21—was identified by French researchers in 1959. Newborn children with DS tend to have a smaller head, shorter neck, and characteristic facial features such as slanting eyes and a flatter face. Mental acuity ranges from 50 to 70 IQ in mild disability cases to less than 35 to 50. As infants grow, one can expect developmental delays in hearing and speech, and slow to mature gross motor skills such as crawling and walking. Basic communication skills and fine motor skills are also affected.

*****

The history of DS and many other disabilities is a difficult one. For example, people with disabilities were among the first targets of eugenics, a pseudoscience promoted by prominent universities and foundations in the 1920s in America. Eugenics presumed that society would be improved by reducing or eliminating people with disabilities, and techniques for doing so were numerous, including sterilization of people who had disabilities and even euthanasia! (Sadly, today in Iceland, a similar mindset now encourages abortion of in-utero babies with genetic disorders determined through early testing. Doctors there have proudly announced that the birth rate of such individuals is now down considerably, a highly engineered percentage.)

Overall, approximately five million people in the United States today have intellectual and developmental disabilities, including DS, autism, cerebral palsy, and all forms of cognitive disabilities. That number would be even higher without screening techniques during pregnancy; even here in the United States an estimated 60 to 80 percent termination rate exists when DS and other conditions are identified prenatally.

For centuries this disadvantaged population has been mostly invisible, warehoused in large inhumane institutions or hidden in family homes. But today, the emphasis on inclusion and integration of people with disabilities in communities, schools, families, homes, and the workplace, is thankfully, shaping different circumstances. The result has been a huge improvement in cognitive and daily living skills, to their benefit and their families. Little did I know as I was exploring this history just how I might fit into this picture.

*****

At first, the scientific information left me baffled. The medical, genetic, and historical content was a lot to process. Yet, I couldn't take in enough. After all, knowledge was the first step in fulfilling my new role as Kennedy's father and protector. On a brighter note, I was reassured by therapists, pediatricians, and other parents with similar concerns that children with Down syndrome have profound relationships with family and caregivers and deep emotional responses. They relate. They learn. They can live truly happy lives. I was told I shouldn't worry. Most of all, these children accept and return love.

But of course they do, I said to myself. *Love affirms they are wanted. As I'd learned from the numerous trials and joys of raising my other children, love transcends all.* I continued to read and seek more facts. Among other things, I discovered that, for centuries, babies born with the condition were doomed from their very first breath. If not weakened by heart damage or other systemic problems, they typically had a short life span of 20 to 25 years or less. Most were relegated to the care of institutions. Secreted away, they were a family's shame, a silent burden.

Just reading this research was painful.

I was shocked to discover that at the start of World War II in the 1930s, Nazi Germany didn't only seek to eliminate gypsies and Jews in its conquest for a dominant Aryan nation, but anyone deemed imperfect as well. Without any compassion, those with intellectual or physical disabilities—some 300,000 souls—were the very first to go. The facts sickened me. To think a modern country could think of individuals with disabilities as less than human was incomprehensible. Incensed and infuriated by what I read, I kept digging, searching for anything encouraging, for every positive thing I could hang onto.

Reaching out into the community, I discovered Arc. (Arc was formerly known as the "Association for Retarded Citizens," a term used before the outdated and offensive term "retarded" was officially retired.) The organization advocated for new ways to keep individuals with intellectual disabilities safe and better cared for, preferably at home. What a connection! Finally, others who cared, and at last a place to turn. I knew I needed to learn more about the organization and get personally involved.

*****

After his birth, Kennedy remained in a hospital for the first couple of weeks, followed by oxygen monitoring at home for the next three months. Luckily, further testing, particularly regarding heart function, proved that his heart was normal. This was a small, saving grace as nearly half of all children born with Down syndrome require surgery to repair holes in their heart following birth.

I was filled with relief at this news, and continued to take one precious day at a time, hiding my worry, burying my concern. All I could do was hope for the future. My deepest fears, often unspoken, continued to be muffled in my attempt to be courageous while seeking every way for my child to thrive.

I remember to this day how I felt, late at night, in the still and peaceful safety of Kennedy's nursery when it was my turn to change his diaper or check his oxygen. I would gaze at him and wonder: *Will you grow up and live a healthy life? Will you ever have friends? Go to a regular school? Love a girl? Marry?* Or simply, my greatest concern of all, *would he ever be able live on his own?* As parents, we both wondered what would happen to him after we were gone. Even more important, when he grew up to be a man, would he feel happy to be alive?

I had no answers. All I knew was, from the first time I saw him, I was determined to provide this child every advantage in the world, plus all the love I could possibly give. We dreamed that one day

Kennedy would be treated no differently than other children, and that he would be mainstreamed into society as much as possible.

That night, alone with him in the nursery, I picked him up and held him close. With unwavering confidence I assured him that he would become a fine human being, productive and independent. I kissed him on the cheek and looked into his long-lashed, dark-blue eyes. He looked back at me and smiled. At that moment, with an even firmer resolve and a feeling forged from the bottom of my heart, I committed the rest of my life to making sure that he would.

So many experiences. So many challenges, areas and avenues I was unaware of that I'd never thought of before. So many things to learn. Knowledge dispels the darkness.

Chapter Five

Understanding the Challenge

*"We must be willing to let go of the life we had planned,
so as to have the life that is waiting for us."*

—*E.M. Forster, novelist*

Once Kennedy's mother and I embraced the reality of our son's condition, I set out to manage the future with a vengeance, seeking out national organizations and local ones, too. Anywhere I could get information that could give me a further edge. Just when I thought I had run out of places to turn, the universe stepped in to direct me to the perfect guide.

Kennedy Lewis and Sophia Kay Whitten as infants.

Dr. Linda S. Crnic, a brilliant, young neuroscientist who worked at the University of Colorado Anschutz Medical Campus in Aurora, east of Denver, entered our lives. She welcomed my questions and offered emotional and academic support. Around the same time, I met a fellow parent of a newborn with Down syndrome, Michelle Sie Whitten, now the celebrated founder and executive director of the hugely successful Global Down Syndrome Foundation in Denver, a world leader in research. Michelle, who had recently given birth to a child with DS, was just as hungry for knowledge and assistance as I was. She was determined to provide the best for her newborn as well.

Kennedy Lewis with Sophia Kay Whitten

Dr. Crnic was not only a neuroscience specialist, but also a highly respected University of Colorado professor of pediatrics and psychiatry. Gifted and compassionate, she served as the director of what is now known as the school's Intellectual and Developmental Disability Research Center. In addition, she led the creation of the new Developmental Psychobiology Research Group at the school. In short, she was a powerhouse and a great mind. Yet, busy as she was, Dr. Crnic had time for everyone, even me. Her interest was people; her goal, the healing of body and soul. In no time at all, I became her devoted initiate, determined to learn what she knew.

Deeply concerned about children with disabilities and their families, Dr. Crnic quickly became my daily source of inspiration. She took the time to explain the biological and scientific underpinnings of Kennedy's condition and what medicine and science had to offer.

"Here's the good news," she shared with me one day over coffee at the hospital. I remember the conversation so clearly, and I took down copious notes as usual. "Persons with Down syndrome, some 350,000 across America, really aren't as disenfranchised as they were before," she said. "We're seeing real progress everywhere. It appears they're finally becoming more and more integrated into society and community organizations, so we have to think positively about their life path."

As she had pointed out earlier, it was already proven that many persons with DS (both adults and children) enjoyed social and recreational activities and, with help, could live truly satisfying lives. Her advice quelled some of my doubts, and gave me reason to feel optimistic about the future.

"On the other hand," she reminded me, "We have to be realistic, Lloyd. Individuals born with Down syndrome have varying degrees of cognitive delays, from very mild to severe, even into adulthood."

That seemed important to me then. It widened the range of possibility, of growth and achievement. It also made me worry.

"And some of these with intellectual or physical disabilities," she continued, "can't communicate using any recognizable language or alternative communication system. In fact, some cannot be understood at all, except by those who know the person well. It's a real disadvantage. Speech can be a lifelong struggle," she added, a grave expression on her face, "And most never find meaningful work."

She was reluctant to add that a shocking number have even suffered some kind of sexual abuse. "But it's true. They can be extremely vulnerable. Some don't even have family or legal guardians, and are incapable of making informed consent decisions for themselves."

The conversation had grown disconcerting, but I begged her to continue.

"I won't kid you, Lloyd," she continued. "Their lives can be difficult, like it or not. So, until things change, be patient. We in the clinical world just have to work with it and do our best to make a difference in their survival."

Her message was understood. I wrote down the word "patience" and underlined it three times. I wanted to believe everything she said. Intellectually, I knew what she was saying, but my heart refused to accept the conflict, the opposing forces, and the difficulty. Those facts she reiterated didn't describe our son—our smiling, laughing, pink-cheeked son. That wasn't his world. At least, not yet. Nor, I hoped, would it ever be. He had us to care for and protect him, for now anyway. He had me as his guardian for as long I lived. Yet I continued to ask, *where would my Kennedy fit in? What does the future hold?*

It was way too early to tell.

*****

For those who are unaware, the genetic research on Down syndrome is daunting, as are the results. Statistics tell the story with numbers that leave no room for doubt. People with a variety of disabilities face many obstacles and many are unable to advocate on their own behalf, even in the simplest of terms. I learned that an average of 71 percent cannot write more than their name or a few single words. A similar percentage need close supervision due to frequent problems in behavior, mental health, major medical, legal, and/or adaptive skills.

In other words, just getting through life every single day for some with intellectual disabilities is a major challenge. Further, too many in this population need frequent assistance with some kind of medical condition that is either chronic or recurrent.

The breadth of this information threw me into a kind of culture shock. Until then, life as I knew it had been the proverbial walk in the park. In my forties, I didn't have or expect any personal medical issues. But the research about Down syndrome made me deeply aware of a hidden reality—something I never really knew existed—the overwhelming world of individuals with physical and intellectual disabilities. And therefore, the long-term expectations for children like our son could only be imagined.

How could I have been so ignorant? Why didn't I know about them, these hidden castaways? But then again, was I any different than most Americans?

These facts joined Dr. Linda Crnic, Michelle Sie and I as allies in a fight against something bigger than all of us. But, we believed, it was not insurmountable. Besides, these myriad challenges didn't define the individuals we cared so much about. They were human beings, after all. They had feelings. They had hearts. And they had our love.

*****

As I think back about Linda Crnic's unwavering dedication to helping me and individuals with Down syndrome through scientific research, I am filled with gratitude. I could have never gotten through those early years without her faith in everything positive and everything I did. By then, she was a well-known author, or coauthor, of dozens of scholarly papers and articles on intellectual disabilities and Down syndrome. She continued to fill me in on all the latest advances. Having gained national recognition in her field, she'd also become a frequent speaker on these topics across the United States and, in fact, around the world. I attended every lecture I could, and hung onto every word, hoping to further absorb what she knew.

Once, I actually accompanied her on a trip to Washington, D.C., to a national conference on Down syndrome. The goal was to help make the case for better support for individual care and research. I actually got a chance to speak my heart to an audience that listened attentively. I wasn't a scientist or a medical expert. I was merely a parent trying to grapple with the rest of my child's fragile life. I remember feeling a tremendous sense of pride when I concluded my talk and the audience stood up and gave me a round of applause confirming that I'd been heard and understood.

It's an understatement to say Linda became my anchor and my guide. I felt as if she held the key to something that, someday, would deliver real improvements in cognition, or at least write a different ending for my son's story. She gave me confidence and she gave me hope. Perhaps it sounds selfish, but Kennedy motivated me to become a scholar in the field and an advocate for the miraculous. With Linda's encouragement, patience, and enthusiasm, I was never discouraged from my dreams.

"Just focus on the progress, Lloyd," she often said, "and don't worry about the setbacks. They're inevitable." She always believed in taking one day at a time. Her most memorable piece of advice was this: "Kennedy will be your teacher as much as you will become his."

How true that turned out to be, and how prophetic as well.

Linda and I both wanted to create a better world for children with disabilities, and learn as much as we could about their growth, success, and chances for a normal or even a semi-normal life. Collaborating with a world-renowned scientist did more for me than offer solace, it was empowering. She made me feel like the key to salvation had to be just around the corner.

"A semi-normal life," she'd said. That line stuck like a mantra. A semi-normal life. Was that too much to ask?

The real question that kept me going and that seemed so essential was simple: Was it possible that someday the world might see these children and adults as equal, and simply accept them for who they really are?

Somehow, I thought it could be done. In fact, I was sure of it. Plus, I figured if you just had the right information, you could affect the outcome in a meaningful way. Knowledge was power. *As much knowledge as you could get.*

Vigilant, I kept on digging.

*****

In 2006, the Sies organized a summit of some of the world's best scientists, including Nobel Laureate Tom Cech, to explore the possibility of breakthrough research for people with Down syndrome. During the summit at the University of Colorado, many of the scientists were skeptical about just how much could be done through science to improve the lives of people with Down syndrome. But at the end of the summit, the scientists had two major reactions: (1) a sense of shock that Down syndrome was the least-funded genetic condition by the National Institutes of Health, and (2) a feeling of confidence that, given recent advances in science and technology, measurable breakthroughs for people with Down syndrome could be accomplished in a short period of time with appropriate levels of funding. This information gave parents like me a reason to hope. That very same year, the idea of the first academic home at the University of Colorado for Down syndrome research was born.

> The search for knowledge opens many doors.
> Everywhere I turned, help was waiting.

Chapter Six

My Son, My Inspiration

"If we're facing in the right direction, all we have to do is keep on walking."

—*Buddhist proverb*

Kennedy with Brooklyn Gilhooly

Kennedy, the infant, began to grow and change. In spite of the obvious setbacks, he was hugely responsive, especially to sound. As a toddler, all kinds of things prompted him to react. Some days, it might have been the kitchen blender on the counter, or the sound of the garage door opening and closing—almost anything with rhythm. Such sounds evoked a physical response; his arms up in the air, feet tapping, body swaying to-and-fro; our child, a *wunderkind*, whirling with life.

His love of music continued. Popular, melodic Disney movie sound tracks, Pixar movies, and simple children's songs on *Sesame Street* were all a reason to move. With the love of rhythm came a love of dancing as well, and Kennedy became quite the dancer! The first time we noticed it was during a Cat Stevens special on PBS, when he was just a toddler. Now, he dances every time he hears music, including one special time at the zoo for an impromptu performance of Pharrell Williams' "Happy" in front of a large crowd gathered near the seal exhibit!

I came to realize that our child Kennedy lived in a different world where everything had the possibility to entertain or at least delight. Affectionate and easily reduced to giggles, it soon became clear that he also lived exclusively in the present, in a state of persistent happiness, not dependent on external circumstances.

What a wonderful personality he'd been gifted with. I could see it already. He was outgoing, friendly, and affectionate, and he touched everyone who met him. Although he struggled with speech, Kennedy's blue eyes still sparkled, and his smile told me everything I needed to know. He was a happy toddler and responded to working with his therapists: speech, occupational, physical, even one for sleep apnea. His mother took him to many of his visits with the pediatrician and other doctors, including overnight sleep studies.

As I watched our son move through the developmental phases I'd always taken for granted in my other children, I had to stretch to become the parent I never was. For example, I couldn't look the other way, not even for a minute, or ever let him out of my sight. Children with Down syndrome are sometimes unaware of physical property boundaries or safety issues, and they can be extremely prone to getting lost.

As an example, a few years ago, he actually did wander away from our house. What an unforgettable day. My heart was filled with terror. I was dumbstruck by the reality that our child had disappeared, and in a mere second! Searching the house everywhere inside, I was beside myself, not knowing where our son had gone. In turned out that in a few brief moments, unbeknownst to us, Kennedy had headed for an open door.

Panic drove me to the front of our house. I headed out the door and turned north, calling his name over and over, trying to stay calm. Then I decided to go towards the church at the end of the street (which involved turning a corner) and, thankfully, I found him inside. That was an experience I will truly never forget. Now, even though he's a young adult, I can't assume that such a danger would lessen, and so I watch him even more carefully, never assuming his whereabouts, never letting him out of earshot or my sight. In fact, we've added a door chime at home that signals when someone comes in *or* goes out.

*****

Early on, Kennedy went to preschool and started kindergarten in a public elementary school program for children with special needs. He spent two years in kindergarten, challenged by all traditional developmental models, especially speech. Speaking clearly for him was extremely difficult. But his outgoing personality, infectious smile, and social skills allowed him to shine. In fact, by the time he was in grade school, Kennedy had many friends. In addition, he'd been invited to appear in numerous fashion shows benefitting charities, always eliciting a genuine and appreciative response from the audience.

At one fashion show held for children who had endured heart surgery, Kennedy was to appear on the runway with a former First Lady of Colorado, Frances Owens. Most of the other models walked out onto the runway in a somewhat moderate or indifferent pace to the sound of a song of their choice. In Kennedy's case, the minute he heard his favorite song (the *Sponge Bob* theme song), he began to run across the stage, hopping up and down in celebration, as the surprised former First Lady ran after him and tried to catch up.

For a kid, Kennedy had, and still has, a great sense of humor. He loves to tell knock-knock jokes, with setups that are fairly understandable, followed by punch lines that usually are unintelligible to all but him, as he quite literally doubles over in laughter. That's the funniest part, watching him enjoy himself. It's contagious. Although not quite yet fully verbal, he also loves to toast his family dinner companions each night, gleefully clinking glasses and exclaiming "Cheers!"

In short, our life is simply richer with Kennedy in it. He is a light unto us all.

At this stage of his life, adolescence, Kennedy reads at a first or second grade level, and does beginning "math." Off and on, he has favored formal attire for school, usually a suit jacket and white dress shirt and black dress shoes, sometimes accompanied by a tie. Dressing this way at times seems very important to him.

In his first year of middle school, he began to have lunch every day with a group of sixth grade girls and a fellow student who also has Down syndrome (a total of six girls and two boys). They have become good friends and he feels comfortable with them. At home, Kennedy shares a room with his younger brother, Aidan, whom he loves very much. He occasionally, however, announces that it's time to pack his backpack or suitcase for a trip to "Hogwarts," or to venture forth to get "married" to his "fiancée," a girl from his former elementary school whom he no longer sees but still adores.

In general, Kennedy is a kind, thoughtful, sympathetic, and wonderful human being. I sometimes say he starts at the place that Buddhist monks strive to get to for decades (Nirvana) and stays there. He's quickly growing into a handsome, broad-shouldered young man, playful and curious. And, just as when he was a very young child, he is outgoing, affectionate, and fun to be around.

*****

In the months following Kennedy's birth, and at the beginning of our relationship as father and son, I relied on Dr. Crnic's reassurance that our child would grow up, slowly, but surely. Sitting, crawling, taking his first steps—all were epic in my view. By the time he could walk, I discovered what it really meant to live in the present, as Kennedy did, and cherish every moment.

I loved this boy unconditionally, as one would hope all parents do—but even more intensely, as if his very life depended on me. Then, as now, I coaxed and encouraged and repeated to him whatever he didn't understand. I forgave every misstep and celebrated every effort. Whatever he needed to learn, I never stopped trying to teach. And in exchange, I learned the first and most important lesson of my role as a parent of a child with a disability—the one Linda Crnic so firmly advised—patience. Patience, above all. And with that understood, the rewards were endless.

Kennedy persevered in ways that left me breathless, his persistence inspiring. My love for him flooded my being as I held his chubby hand or steadied his stance. A big hug at the end of every accomplishment, no matter how small, did wonders for us both, and still does. And yet, in my deepest heart, I still worried if this happy, courageous, and exceptional little boy would always stay so full of joy.

Persons with disabilities are humbling. They teach us to be grateful. Their honesty is incomparable. Get to know them and learn.

Chapter Seven

A Peek into the Future

"Each contact with a human being is so rare, so precious, one should preserve it."

—*Anaïs Nin, novelist*

Among other concerns I had when Kennedy was a toddler was this: *What would life be like when he became an adult?* An independent adult, hopefully. I think the issue of assuming some kind of independence has to be the biggest fear all parents of children with disabilities share. For some reason, I couldn't picture it; I had nothing to go on. But that ambiguity disappeared the very first time I walked into an arc Thrift Store in Denver back in 2005, shortly after being invited to join the company. It was a major turning point.

Like most secondhand shops, the store was an emporium of donated items and gently used goods, filled with the kinds of things some us no longer use or need. The building seemed to be a renovated grocery store, one of the company's older locations on the east side of town.

Situated on busy Colfax Avenue, a street that bisects Denver east to west, it served a wide variety of people, from hard working locals so challenged as to barely make ends meet, to some living on welfare staying in local motels. That was the demographic in this area back then, filled with many citizens who were just trying to get by. Other types of customers included blue-collar workers residing in small homes and bungalows, as well young singles and married couples who liked to visit thrift stores to seek out vintage treasures.

Looking around, I have to say that the retail property itself was clearly aging. The space was very much like some of the hand-me-downs for sale in the store—worn and frayed. It had older linoleum floors, florescent lighting, and bolted iron racks of secondhand clothing. I'd never been in a thrift store before and it was a new experience for me. At the time, it just wasn't the kind of place I would ever have thought to buy anything. Then, secondhand wasn't my style. But once through that door on that remarkable and memorable day, everything changed.

It wasn't the array of items piled high around me, or the needy shoppers filling grocery carts with used garments, tools, and toys. No. What was so memorable was meeting the first, employed, full-grown adult with Down syndrome I had ever encountered—a man named Garnons Muth.

Garnons, then forty-two years old, was a backroom employee whose job was hanging lady's clothing. He tackled his job with enthusiasm and a great attitude. His immediate, warm smile said it all. As I stepped forward he said "Hi. I'm Garnons."Once introduced, he treated me as if we were old friends.

*****

Garnons' broad face had some of the features that can result from Down syndrome, such as a noticeable slanting of eyes that peered through thick glasses resting on chubby cheeks. The man was direct and not the least bit self-conscious, and I made an instant connection. (Oddly enough—I was self-conscious.) But I was touched by his friendliness and direct gaze.

Looking around him in the store, I saw all the things people didn't have a use for, or want anymore, and I assessed the eclectic assembly of thrift store employees working there as well. Good people. Hardworking people. I thought to myself, *So maybe this is where the people who are different and who have their own challenges feel most comfortable.* A place where everything isn't perfect or new anymore. And yet, a place where people care.

In spite of my new position as a consultant to arc Thrift (but before I became its CEO), the idea that persons with Down syndrome, or any other kind of disability, could hold regular jobs in public places seemed foreign to me. Unheard of, really. Standing in front of Garnons, I realized, why not? Here were the kind of jobs they could easily handle, in a safe and secure environment.

What had a minute earlier seemed nebulous suddenly became clear. This might just be the future, at least for some. Maybe it wasn't the swankiest address, but here at this store, people like Garnons Muth had jobs and an employer who welcomed them each and every day they came to work.

Buoyed by this realization, I began to reassess all the months of worry and concern I'd endured since Kennedy's birth, agonizing about his uncertain future. There *were* options after all, *real opportunities* for inclusion. Garnons was one of just ten persons with disabilities originally hired by the thrift chain, a far cry from the future paradigm that would see that number of employed persons change radically. Meeting him face-to-face marked a new beginning. Seeing him smile as he worked reassured me. Something in my head and heart rallied, and opened the door to a new way of thinking. I was seeing things in a relative way, justifying thoughts about Kennedy's life—positive thoughts, imagining useful work outside the long-term shelter of our home. Garnons Muth was a living reality, his employment a conquest of my deepest fears. By the time we left the store, I was filled with excitement and encouraged by the all-encompassing idea that this world surely had a place for everyone, including adults with Down syndrome.

*****

That night I held Kennedy in my arms as I read him a bedtime story. He loved books (just as I always did, and still do) and adored looking at the pictures while I explained what was happening on each page. Then, as now, our son was noticeably behind on most milestones, developing along the typical lines of a child with Down syndrome. Communication was still difficult and his coordination uneven. But it didn't matter to me. Those things didn't define him. Both of us now lived in the present and took things day by day.

Although I read to him often, I was never sure exactly what he understood. But as I shared his favorite story with him that night, I could already see him in my mind, tackling his first job, whatever it was. I hugged him closer than ever, with a profound realization that he might be different in many ways, but he might also one day be part of something that truly mattered, working for people who really cared.

Do what you love with a full heart
and the money will follow. Happy
employees in any business increase
productivity which increases profits,
including employees with disabilities.

Chapter Eight

Garnons Muth - An Adult with Down Syndrome

"If we have no peace, it is because we have forgotten that we belong to each other."

—*Mother Teresa, nun and missionary*

Consider the human body: four limbs, 600 muscles, 100,000 miles of arteries, 230 movable joints, and 2.5 trillion red blood cells. The numbers overwhelm the imagination. Deep within every one of those cells lays a specific combination of intertwining molecules with 46 chromosomes—a major part of our DNA, our past, and in some ways, our very future.

Beyond any explanation, an unexpected shift in the cosmos of creation results in one out of 800 individuals born with the presence of an extra copy of chromosome 21, the very smallest one. Born with this genetic difference, those who have this gene sometimes bear identifiable, telltale signs—eyes slightly slanted, faces flattened or rounded with muscles more relaxed, and brain functioning impaired to some degree. Depending on circumstances, fortune and fate define the rest. But the question arises: Are these individuals to be excluded from a life fulfilled?

Absolutely not.

Former First Lady of Colorado Frances Owens and Garnons.

In truth, they're not so different from us, after all. In fact, any one of them could teach us a thing or two. I know they can. Our arc Thrift employee Garnons Muth is a great example.

*****

Garnons loves bowling. He doesn't just go bowling every week; he makes sure everyone he works with at the Colfax store knows all about it. When he comes in to work the morning after a bowling night, he announces his scores over the PA system to the cheers of all the employees, and most of the store customers, too. That's celebrating. That's sharing. And it's fine.

Did I mention exciting? That too! You bet it is.

Garnons' happiness matters, and to all the people who are like family at the arc Thrift store on East Colfax in Denver, it matters a lot. On February 19, 2016, Garnons celebrated his fifty-third birthday, making him one of the longest-employed persons at arc Thrift in Colorado. That birthday marked twenty-eight years as a loyal, faithful, and productive part of the arc Thrift team.

It's worth pointing out that Garnons is a noticeably meticulous groomer and a snappy dresser, too. He wears high-waisted trousers and high-top, white socks. Garnons has grown a subtle but dashing moustache, reinforcing the fact that he's something of a lady's man—he's definitely not shy around girls. And, oh yes, he loves any flavor of Jell-O and old-time radios. In the world of individuals born with Down syndrome, Garnons leads a successful and rewarding life.

*****

For most of his career, Garnons' job consisted of moving lady's clothing from a sorting table onto hangers three days a week for an eight-hour day with a break for lunch. And Garnons loves what he does. His speech may not be perfectly clear, but he chats while he works. He knows every employee by name and is quick to quip and tease.

Former employee Rachel Thomas and Garnons.

A certificate of appreciation for Garnons.

On the day of his birthday in 2016, various arc Thrift store managers and employees came upstairs to a brightly decorated break area to share in a company-sponsored luncheon (Chinese food, Garnons' favorite) and enjoy a personalized birthday cake. Balloons filled the air. Volunteers assisted from a local nonprofit on the retail floor so that individuals downstairs could leave their posts. So much more than a birthday party, this celebration was an affirmation of everything good and important, both in Garnons' life and the company's. Call it people-caring-about people. arc Thrift goes out of its way to acknowledge milestones and birthdays—the things that count, moreover, the things that matter.

*****

Garnons' longevity is a triumph in itself because individuals with Down syndrome historically have short life spans. It might be his winning personality that keeps him going; his kindness, his positive attitude, and his sheer love of people that make him so fulfilled. But it might also be because he has a reason to get up most days, and he knows where he fits in and where he is accepted and loved.

Garnons is an extremely good listener. If he intuits sadness or depression, he doesn't hang back. He hugs perfect strangers or employees who seem to be having a bad day. Back in 2005 when I first met Garnons, I saw in him someone that my own son might become. I saw someone with an engaging personality who has a profound impact on his peers, someone who radiates joy and evokes positivity from others. Now, years later, and especially on this momentous birthday, my first impressions were confirmed.

Isn't that what we all want, I asked myself. To be like Garnons Muth and make others around us feel better, make others feel accepted and loved?

That birthday party, one of many at our company, left me wistful. I gifted Garnons with a certificate of appreciation and a fun memento: a small acrylic case with a miniature bowling alley and bowling pins suspended inside. As I headed down the stairs on the way to my next meeting, I realized that it wasn't the first time I found myself wondering: *Who, in fact, among us had the disability?*

> Our Ambassadors make the invisible visible—
> the greatest gift to another human being.
> They confirm that persons with disabilities
> have value. That's what arc Thrift does best.

Chapter Nine

Fighting the Good Fight

"Some men see things as they are and ask why.
Others dream things that never were and ask why not."

—George Bernard Shaw, playwright

At the time of my pivotal visit to the Colfax store in 2005, I had already developed a personal relationship with the local company called arc Thrift, the nonprofit operating not only that location, but sixteen other stores as well. I'd seen an ad for the company earlier that year on TV and realized that the CEO was actually an old friend of mine with whom I had worked at IBM years earlier. Small world! I had no idea he was employed there.

We connected, had lunch, and he tapped into my passion for "everything Down syndrome." He couldn't get over it. What a coincidence! Over a series of several more meetings, he began to recruit me for the company as a financial consultant, saying that they needed some help in budgetary planning and product sourcing.

I was flattered. It felt good to be needed. At the same time, my own employment with a high-tech startup near Boulder was becoming increasingly less of a focus. My interests were now centering on advocacy for my son, and the idea of assisting arc Thrift in some way seemed an opportune chance to realize these emerging interests. Working for a nonprofit clearly supported my rapidly shifting values, and felt so much closer to home—closer to my changing ideals.

My ideals?

Who was I kidding? In a way, I had never had any ideals besides the obvious—making money. Was it possible that after all this time, for whatever reasons, I was beginning to form a respectable credo that would carry me forward, over and above providing a living for my family? Dare I say I was beginning to see the world differently?

The offer to step in as Chief Financial Officer came sooner than I expected and was an irresistible invitation. Although I was an outsider and completely new to the nonprofit world, my friend suggested that I join the administrative team right away and help reinforce the business end of things. Would I quit my other job and come on board?

The opportunity seemed more than ideal. It would utilize my best skills while challenging me to source new ones. It connected me to the community of persons with disabilities and gave me a platform to seek more information on their behalf. But before I could take my rightful place at the helm and reach for new heights, I unexpectedly lost one essential piece of my newly formed universe. The shocking news seemed surreal.

I remember feeling completely numb when I learned that my beloved colleague, Dr. Linda S. Crnic— Colorado University's most respected professor, scientist, and global change maker, as well as my mentor, personal friend, and guiding light—had suffered a massive stroke and lethal head injuries while riding a bicycle during a vacation in Europe. She was only fifty-six years old when the accident occurred. Rushed to an ambulance and then a local hospital, emergency services were not able to revive her. My most important ally and constant source of inspiration was gone.

Linda's death left me feeling incredibly isolated and alone. Overnight, the future loomed unsure, reawakening the same kind of feelings that plagued me when I first began to search for answers for Kennedy, not knowing which way to go. Without Linda's unwavering guidance, the road ahead seemed dark indeed, and unwelcome pangs of self-doubt and fear reappeared.

*****

There's an old question that plagues every warrior. "Just exactly how does one walk into a lion's den?"

(With eyes open, one would think.)

I began my new job warily, hoping to fully understand just what I had gotten into. Like most new hires, my initial impressions of arc Thrift were that the company was doing well. As a consultant, I hoped to impress my new employers with my financial expertise and enthusiasm. At the start, they recruited me to take a close look at donations and fiscal issues, which were major concerns. But once I became CFO, I assumed some operations responsibilities as well. I handled the telemarketing and oversaw the warehouse, a whole lot more than I had bargained for. I found myself juggling priorities and testing personalities. But as a result, I began to see the bigger picture, including the cracks and the shortfall; in fact, I saw all the problems everywhere, even ones I'm sure they weren't ready for me to see. As much as I didn't want to say so, things definitely didn't line up as they should have.

By midsummer, it became clear that numerous initiatives implemented months earlier were not panning out. One of those was a plan to change how we produce "product" for the stores—that is, how we sort and prioritize donations. My predecessor had hoped to cut costs by processing products for two locations from one store. We were constantly sorting these for sales that best suited the season, as well as for quality, price, and demand. Keep in mind, each store receives up to 12,000 pounds of items a day, some 20 to 30,000 pieces of cloth or hard goods. The so-called cost-cutting plan wasn't working; in fact, we were losing money.

As I was trying to sort out the dilemma, the president left the company. I stepped up my own efforts, urging my managers to ramp up operations and marketing. We were all encouraged as retail sales begin to climb. But the further I got into the internal affairs, the less I liked what I saw. Several issues arose—relationship questions, issues unresolved. It became clear that a change in top management across the stores was needed. The arc Thrift Board of Directors agreed for me to take the reins and become the interim CEO by October, and next, step into a full-time, permanent leadership position by December of that year.

Incredible! Who would have thought? I should have been excited by the offer, but in my heart I wasn't sure I had the necessary support. In fact, I knew I didn't. The atmosphere around me was filled with mistrust.

I remember one of my board members confiding in me: "Lloyd, I hate to say it," he said, "but you just don't have our managers' confidence. Most of them at the various stores who know you don't like your style; they think you're the wrong choice. You move too fast. You're critical, impatient, and arrogant. Seriously, that's the word out on the floor. And you have no retail experience. If you accept this position, I guarantee you, it's not going to be easy."

Sadly, I knew he was right. My lack of thrift and retail experience and tough demeanor had started things off on the wrong foot, and I wasn't sure how to fix it. But I would not be deterred. The old Lloyd always thought he could forge his way through necessary changes by sheer determination, and so I fought harder, put on my game face, and headed into the fray.

Isn't that the way I always got what I wanted?

It was, but this time around, by doing so, I caused some doubt in my leadership style among the team members. It was discouraging, and time to consider another strategy.

I tried to slow down, soft-pedal my demands, and get to know the individual managers personally, taking them into my confidence. I worked with them in groups as well, tapping into their own strengths. Thankfully, by the end of my first year as president/CEO, the financial picture at arc Thrift had changed from worrisome, declining, year-over-year sales to a significant, measurable, and positive increase. My approach was working. Things were looking up.

Not bad for a newcomer in foreign seas towing a lifeboat, right? I just needed everyone to climb on board and help me sail. But more importantly, behind the numbers, what I really wanted to do was to get to work on a different priority altogether—the employment of persons with disabilities, what I perceived as a very important factor in our future growth.

I kept thinking, *Why not them? Why not? Why not? Why couldn't we build the heart of this business around improving these people's daily lives?*

That's what really mattered to me. That's what I wanted more than anything.

Dream big. Aim High. Be the
change you want to see.

Chapter Ten

Education Is the Key

"If you're not the hero of your own story, then you're missing the whole point of your humanity."

—Steve Maraboli, *speaker*

The idea of hiring more employees with disabilities became an obsession. It was all I could think of, night and day. *If ten employees could work for us, why not a hundred? Why not 200?*

At the beginning of my tenure in 2005, the company mission was all about improving production "efficiency" and the way we did business, processing the huge volume of goods we took in and pushed out. Until I stepped in, the other previous goal had been to fund advocacy programs for Arc chapters. In fact, until I took over, most of our current employees did not really understand the larger picture, the one about including more and more individuals with disabilities in our workforce on a much larger scale. But, over time, with my enthusiasm, eventually that became almost *all* that anyone was talking about.

I tried to make it clear that what I wanted to do was improve our business *and* set a new business example. I began to see the model more definitively. Employing persons with intellectual and developmental disabilities would be a wonderful way to raise morale. Everyone in business knows that raising morale is closely related to raising productivity, and that, in turn, improves revenue. It was too simple. It was beautiful. It absolutely had to work.

In the beginning, I believe I developed the passion for this idea because I thought it was the right thing to do—and further, because I was a father who cared about the future of his son. That hasn't changed, not a whit. And at that point in my leadership, I also believed wholeheartedly that these special employees might be the real key to our success, and we to theirs.

After all, I had seen for myself that persons with disabilities were loyal and productive. They appreciated their jobs and came to work on time, faithfully. They were people who worked for more than a paycheck. They worked for a purpose, and they wanted to make a difference.

I pressed on, getting the word out to all the conduits (families, friends, others in the disability community) who brought these individuals to our attention. "Bring them on," I encouraged. "We have room for them all."

I knew at that point we had a chance to set something truly important in motion, something very few had attempted on such a large scale before. I couldn't stop thinking about little Kennedy and how fast he was growing up. Before long, he too would need to make some choices. I was committed to being ready for him, figuratively and literally. Moreover, I wanted the world to be ready for him, too.

I needed to be very sure that the future would be receptive to my child and his needs would not go unmet.

Somehow, without me even realizing it, my reason for living and Kennedy's had become one. I decided to emphasize personally and publicly the mission of the company—employing those with disabilities, as a better business practice, in fact, as our company mantra. It was both a matter of policy and one of continuity, to be embraced more and more fully by the company over time.

The idea was met with open arms by most. Some, even with enthusiasm. Those who doubted me would have to be won over, but it was a challenge worth taking on.

In the end, I decided to stay the course, no matter what the cost, and pursue our disabilities employment program with a vengeance. It was *the* priority. The candidates were ready, of that there was no doubt. The bigger question was this: *What else could we provide to enrich their lives and self-esteem, and their ability to perform their jobs?*

Here's where it gets interesting. I realized we might have to create a program—a kind of post-secondary program, not connected to job training. So, with the exponential expansion of our employees with disabilities, we made a decision to supplement their employment with a program called "arc University." Total, overall life education. The possibilities were mindboggling.

We could do this; I felt certain we could. The idea for the school and its vast curriculum possessed me. It was the missing piece, for sure. Just like raising Kennedy, one success begat the next. One step at a time, like Linda Crnic had so much earlier advised. We decided to create a year-round learning opportunity for any individual who needed it and build it out, one subject, one mentor, one teacher, and one volunteer at a time.

I began to dream of a new paradigm, a larger picture than I'd ever, ever imagined before. In my mind, I began to construct a brave new world where retail stores of any kind, not just ours, could benefit from persons with disabilities contributing to their success based on training *the whole person*. It seemed the perfect approach. In fact, the *only* one. I could hardly wait to see this brand-new world come into being.

Believe, re-commit every single day, and never let anyone deter you from your goal.

Chapter Eleven

The Man in the Mirror

"If you want to make the world a better place, take a look at yourself, then make a change."

—*Michael Jackson, singer*

As time went on, Linda Crnic's untimely passing left a hole in the lives of many, especially the Down syndrome community. Following her death, her immediate absence seemed impossible to fill. For a time, I felt inconsolable, unable to process the reality. And it haunted me. I turned away from the world of research and took a hiatus from my relentless study, seeking solace in the world of advocacy instead.

In the midst of that deeply painful memory, and many other shifts taking place around me—especially the company's changing corporate culture—it became clear that I was changing, too. I had become a better listener; more empathetic, and more compassionate. I took a personal interest in every employee we had, learning most of their names and individual stories. I started making quarterly rounds to visit every single store along the Front Range, sometimes driving more than a hundred miles each way to confer with managers and employees alike, implementing recognition awards and giving out tokens for accomplishments and to those with the most positive attitude.

These visits gave me a chance to see everyone at least four times a year or more, and, even now, I am told that the stores actually looked forward to these events, scheduling them with sincere appreciation.

Understand this: I don't work independently. The team members of arc Thrift comprise a very big entity. I'm just the captain of the team. Most of my senior managers grew up in the business and understand it thoroughly, inside and out. They help assess the very best fits in the workforce. Our criteria for hiring employees at every level is based on the candidate's commitment to our mission and their abilities as well as their performance. It's the platform we all stand on. And as we've learned over time, regardless of their disabilities, training new hires for every level of the workforce turned out to be less of a challenge than we ever imagined. It's all about acceptance, respect, and support.

As I continued to get to know my senior managers better, our solidarity strengthened and our success began to skyrocket. Earnings didn't just double, they began to triple. Among my top management personnel is Shelly Wilson, one of four District Managers. She is a no-nonsense, enthusiastic, attractive woman in her mid-fifties who exudes a good measure of authority and an even larger one of love.

Shelly has been with us for ten years and often works at our Centennial location, a relatively new and spacious store in suburban southeast Denver. In her own words, "This job is the absolute best position I have ever had in my entire life. When you see these individuals change, and see them take pride in their work, it's so gratifying. They always want to do a good job. In fact, my own life has changed. We work for these employees as hard as they work for us. But when you get home at the end of the day, you know you've affected someone's life. That really matters. It makes it all worthwhile."

One of her store managers, David Aldrich, added, "I love this job, too, for all the same reasons. Plus, you never have the same day twice!"

Something at this store is clearly working since this location has seen major increases in donations and customer count every single year. Especially return customers! In fact, the store is substantially over their sales quota at the time of this writing. Without a doubt, our growing workforce of employees with disabilities is making an enormous contribution: productivity, a positive environment, and increased profits. Who could possibly ask for more?

*****

My own job responsibilities have grown from finding new store opportunities to investing capital in new stores, setting revenue targets, developing expense budgets, and making healthy investments. I also visit the warehouses, trucking depots, and call center. Each year, I oversee the donation of 150 tons of food to the Colorado Volunteers of America. (Yes, we do that too, helping support the VOA. We make sure nothing goes to waste.)

Most important to me, however, is getting around to meeting the employees, those with disabilities and those without. I find it fascinating to review who we consider for jobs here; every case is so unique.

Allow me to introduce you to Seth Weshnak, our thirty-one year-old cashier at the arc Thrift JCRS Shopping Center store in Lakewood, Colorado.

Upon meeting, you would not surmise that Seth has any challenges whatsoever. He is bright, outgoing, articulate, and expressive. He appears to love people and takes his job quite seriously, an important quality considering finances are involved. But Seth has Asperger's syndrome, identified as part of the autism spectrum disorder, also known as ASD.

Seth Weshnak

According to medical experts, Asperger's generally manifests without any extreme intellectual disabilities. Outward characteristics of a person with this syndrome can include poor social skills, a lack of empathy, an inability to form friendships, a preference for routine, a tendency toward literal interpretations, and a strong ability for pattern recognition, often resulting in high math skills. Its demands are enough to prevent many who have this condition from succeeding in normal jobs.

"I used to work at McDonald's before I came here," said Seth. "It really didn't work out. I didn't fit in. But arc Thrift is a different story. Everyone here was so welcoming; I love my job. The store where I work is like my family."

"Seth has grown into a highly respected man here," said Scott Jeffers, his store manager. "I care a great deal about him. It's been amazing to watch him grow into this position. He's so responsible, he even does his own budgeting now. He's working full time, which at arc Thrift is 32 hours a week. He's amazing to watch; he has incredible math skills."

"I like to think," said Seth, "that I'm the last person our customers might see or talk to before leaving the store since I work the check-out desk. That means a lot to me. I might be their total experience here. I like to have fun and give them a 'hard time', too. (For fun, of course.) One thing I often ask them to do is to 'round up their total'. Almost no one says no. I've calculated that we make at least $300 a year extra because of that!"

When asked if all the chaos of a customer's shopping cart laid out on his counter doesn't throw him off, he smiled. "That doesn't bother me. As long as all the change in my cash drawers is lined up properly, I am okay."

*****

My operations team members continue to look for ways to streamline and strengthen our operations. We like to hold a monthly managers' meeting that includes corporate staff. The agenda takes almost a full day. I open the meeting with a survey of the mission and re-emphasize its goals and success. I remind everyone to focus on the employees with disabilities and get to know these workers personally, on their own terms. Find out who they are, what they like and need. Communicate. I urge the managers and department heads to be patient and understanding, whatever it takes.

At the meetings, I also try to have conversations with one of our employees with disabilities in front of our 50 or so managers. I ask them to talk about their jobs, lives, hopes, dreams, friends, and more. I've been doing this on a monthly basis for the last 13 years. It's a good way for our managers to get a deeper sense of people with disabilities and our mission.

I close the morning by asking for presentations from each of the support departments: accounting, IT, marketing, and all others. Then lunch and breakout sessions are dedicated to solving the challenges we face. I like to promote healthy discussions. These sessions are a good way to help teams integrate, while helping to take management to the next level.

I'll be honest when I say I may not be the world's most brilliant CEO, but I think I've discovered how to get the most out of people. Our growth and profits attest to that. In essence, I always remind, we're all working to make a difference in people's lives—an absolutely inestimable end.

Because arc Thrift is a nonprofit entity, the company naturally has a board of directors with members who serve three-year terms and help define our public persona, an important part of the picture. Along with my input, they develop long-term strategy and policy, and they secure the financial health of the company via quarterly board meetings. These people are truly the wind beneath my wings, a reliable force when it comes to goals, program implementation, and financial support.

In addition, several committees meet at least quarterly: public relations, finance, audit, personnel, and executive. It's my job to review their meeting minutes thoroughly and give feedback. This way we're all keeping up and staying abreast.

All of our board members are asked to contribute financially to arc Thrift, and they do so willingly. We're so grateful for that. In a sense, I answer daily to all of them, and because of these enormously dedicated volunteers, my job and responsibilities have grown dramatically over the course of my tenure. But I love what I do, and am proud to say that, most days, I feel as if I'm captain of a ship that could sail the seven seas. And together, no matter what, we could weather any storm.

Stand up for what matters to you.
Stick to your principles and never quit.

Chapter Twelve

Working for a Purpose

"Every single time you help somebody stand up, you are helping humanity rise."

—*Steve Maraboli, speaker*

There's an old saying I've heard often in the corporate world. "Leadership is never taken; it's given." Establishing myself successfully at arc Thrift required a hefty series of trials and tribulations, ascending a gradual upward slope until my footing was secure and I felt respected and sure of my place.

As sales climbed and profits increased in my first year as CEO, we began to search for new locations. Even as the overall U.S. economy ebbed or accelerated, our sales continued to grow. Stores increased in square footage and prestige, and we were beginning to locate stores in better neighborhood strip malls and shopping centers. Facelifts and interior makeovers made us competitive with regular retail boutiques. We improved lighting and used newer styles of display racks.

But it wasn't always easy. In those tough early years when sales were in decline and we were cash poor, we had many challenges to properly operate the business. The restructuring, part of which I've shared, took time and patience. Twelve years later, I am proud to say that we can boast over ten successive record years for profitable revenue, as well as an increase in earnings, customers, and product collected and produced.

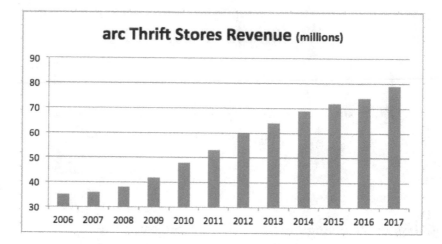

At the onset, as determined by my management team, production was the key—that is, the procurement of both hard and soft goods. It became clear, for example, that clothing sales had to increase, and they did. Under my watch, on average, we now collect and process more than 100 million clothing and other items annually, either for retail sale or bundled export to countries that recycle these goods.

More important, our commitment to employees with disabilities increased. Even without the late Linda Crnic's generous counsel, I found other professionals who helped construct our exemplary employee training program called Working for a Purpose, something you'll learn more about later in this book. We didn't just hire people who needed jobs; we helped cultivate the important sense of inclusion and independence they so desperately sought. As was so well-said by Scott Jeffers, the manager of our JCRS store in Lakewood, "Many of us learned what we know now through on-the-job training, discovering for example, how to be more accepting and tolerant."

It's important to note that any disciplinary action with respect to our employees with disabilities can only be considered with my approval. Not doing the job may be due to many reasons. Together, managers and myself look at the larger picture to see what is really going on, and how we can help. Working with people with disabilities, there is a tremendous need for flexibility, support, and accommodation. We make sure that our rules allow for individual consideration.

*****

In a short time, my role as CEO found further recognition, and I began to accept invitations to take part in other community leadership positions. Initially, I got involved in advocacy for Down syndrome scientific research. Not long after that, the invitation came to speak at the National Down Syndrome Congress Convention on the East Coast, where I actually met a number of people from Denver. A year later, I met with the Director of the National Institutes of Health, followed by meetings with research scientists at the University of Colorado, some from the very same lab where famed scientist/professor Thomas R.Cech did his research. The recognition felt affirming and rewarding. It was hard to imagine, but our work was in the limelight and I was beginning to give back as much as I had been given.

It means a great deal to me to say that another community leader, Julie Reskin, Executive Director of the Colorado Cross-Disability Coalition, has been a big supporter. I joined her board in 2009 and now serve as co-chair. The mission of the coalition is to advocate for social justice for people with all types of disabilities. This is what "cross-disability" means. This includes, but is not limited to, people with intellectual and developmental disabilities. The Coalition helps individuals who have problems with different systems—such as health care—and they work to improve these systems. Sometimes that means changing a rule or law, and sometimes it means educating people, including people with disabilities. One issue the Coalition is tackling is employment as far too few people with disabilities are working.

"One of the mistakes in general that I see people with disabilities make," said Julie during a recent interview for this book, "is not asking for a reasonable accommodation that they need to be successful at their jobs. What arc Thrift has shown is that by teaching employees skills such as advocacy, their employees learn to ask for accommodations. Most employers are happy to provide these minor adjustments, but too often the employee does not ask, the employer does not know, and problems that could have been averted grow. We do not want to hire out of pity—we want to hire people with disabilities because it is good business. Lloyd Lewis is a great model of an ethical business person and runs his company in a moral way, especially when it comes to how you treat people. He truly 'walks the walk.' Most of all, he has high expectations and that's good for everyone."

"arc Thrift's ability to raise money for advocacy programs that serve those with disabilities is incredible," Julie continued. "They have become highly respected in the advocacy world. Lloyd does not just rest on his laurels, but uses his considerable business acumen to benefit others in the disability community. He has been a significant mentor to me and helped me turn the Cross-Disability Coalition around. His leadership has been instrumental on our board. He is well known as a top-notch board member and many others are asking him to be on their boards as well. I have been so honored not only that he was willing to join, but that he has stuck it out."

*****

As my reputation grew as an advocate and spokesperson for the Down syndrome community, I was invited to serve on the Colorado Governor's Human Services Transition Team. It seemed as if, wherever I looked, new doors were opening and new organizations were inviting me in. My life was a whirlwind—and still is—but I thrived on the opportunity to lead and connect in such meaningful ways. Indirectly, it was all additional training for the larger role I had committed to fulfill.

Clearly, I'd left the corporate finance world behind me forever (and the one-time, tempting lure of over 100,000 stock options), never to return. For better or worse, nonprofits and the cause of individuals with disabilities had become my battleground. Yet, in spite of all my recognition and success, and my influence in the DS world, things weren't as perfect as I wished. I hated to admit it, but things in my personal life weren't working too well.

Due in part to my commitment to all things Down syndrome—or my lack of time, or my incessant drive due to my old fear of not succeeding, or changes over the years in my own personality—behind the scenes, my relationship with Kennedy's mother was failing. I couldn't make it work anymore. Home life became increasingly unmanageable for me and I decided to end my relationship with her. As difficult as that seemed at the time, it was my only recourse. By then, my other children were old enough to understand, or at least I hoped they were. Kennedy and his new brother Aidan would continue to have us both as their Mom and Dad, of course, just separately. I vowed that fact would never change. But the break with Kennedy's mom on a personal level was just one more rung in my journey of self-realization, wherein an exacting, new set of values that I had begun to embrace would determine everything I did.

Sometimes being true to oneself is the hardest thing. But it's the place you have to start from every single day.

Chapter Thirteen

Looking Back

"The miracle of man is not how far he has sunk but how magnificently he has risen."

—*Robert Ardrey, playwright*

Writing a memoir of any kind provides a new lens with which to look at one's life. Looking back, random pieces begin to fit together in entirely different ways, and then, the previously indiscernible details of the bigger picture start to be revealed.

To fully appreciate who I am today and how I got here, it's important to understand that for me, the 1990s, long before I was hired by arc Thrift, were all about success—about climbing that overrated corporate career ladder as rapidly as possible. That hectic period, which now seems almost alien, is what makes this era all the more remarkable.

Like almost everyone else I knew back then, I was part of the "Me Generation," determined to reinvent the world and harness it to our personal goals. Most of us had come out of college and pursued success with a vengeance, seeking as many shortcuts as possible. We would acquire material wealth, ascend to the top no matter what, and waste no time in doing so. The young guns of the financial industry in which I had worked all had much in common—self-fulfillment, sometimes regardless of the cost.

So, when I found myself sitting with a friend at an outdoor café near Boulder, Colorado, that life-changing summer afternoon in 2003 just before Kennedy was born, I had the feeling everything was possible. I had come far rather quickly, and looked at my life as a series of battles and conquests, with a few failures to haunt me. For the most part, I felt like I was winning in measurable increments. Looking out at our towering Rocky Mountains, I sipped a glass of local Colorado beer and mused upon the way those faraway heights seemed to infuse everything around them with strength and grandeur. They reflected my turbulent confidence, or maybe, in truth, it was my lack thereof, and the endless lure of challenge.

At the time, my family and I were living in a bedroom community near Boulder, an area famous for intellectual tumult and the campuses of major think tanks. Some of the world's greatest minds were just a stone's throw away, both at the University of Colorado and other alternative centers of education. So were technology giants like Storage Tek and similar mega-employers. As mentioned earlier, I myself was working for a local tech startup and hoping to go international with our new product soon.

I was approaching fifty, and had an MBA in finance from the University of Chicago's Graduate School of Business. For twenty years, I had enjoyed a long financial career with companies such as IBM, where I'd served as a senior financial analyst. Successive jobs included director of finance for a publicly traded company, controller, and then CFO for the aforementioned startup, which was ultimately sold to Micron. My former employers all defined me as a bulldog— someone who was ambitious and didn't let go. What's more, they all knew I was determined to succeed, regardless of the cost.

With a series of good connections, I'd made an upward trajectory through the corporate world, despite some setbacks. I was self-centered and defined life by material wealth. In so many ways, I know now I was misguided; determined to get rich, but not build a better world. I was shallow and unaware, unabashedly disconnected. In fact, like the characters in *The Great Gatsby* by F. Scott Fitzgerald, a favorite novel of mine, I lived in a world of grand illusions. I rarely, if ever, had a self-reflective moment while I pursued a fast track in the financial sector, defining progress with more pay, a bigger house, and more perks. As a result, I had some serious setbacks. My personal life suffered. A first marriage ended, then a second.

I thought I knew exactly where I was going; but for all kinds of reasons, I just couldn't take anyone I loved along for the ride. I sensed eventually that the real source of my conflicts was deep within myself. In fact, long after that period ended, and well into my tenure with arc Thrift, privately, the question that plagued me was, *How could I overcome my own self-doubts to help people who were so very much in need of my help?*

I can confess now that I couldn't seem to shake my insecurity. I was hesitant and fearful. Growing up, I fought a self-image as a shy kid who lacked self-confidence and a true sense of who he was. I was the one who, in his early teens managed to deliver newspapers and sell Fuller Brush products door-to-door to complete strangers, but otherwise, couldn't face authority figures or look them in the eye.

Although I was raised mostly in Tacoma, Washington, we moved around a lot to various cities and states, and I found it hard to integrate, coping with different neighborhoods, different schools. I tried in vain to hide my fear of authority, but it followed me into adolescence where I learned that my growing interest in sports was the only respite from my nagging self-doubt.

Engaging in sports helped me hide my feelings, quell my anxiety, and learn to revere athletic competition instead. Slowly, I created a different version of myself, one that couldn't be hurt and couldn't be pushed around. Over time, I discovered that sometimes, if you push, you get what you want. And if you push hard enough, you win. But when I didn't win, I managed to find an answer for every failure, even when I sank to my lowest point. And yet, I always believed the only way was up. Just move on. Start over. Run with the pack.

Following college, I perceived myself as a winner in an era of faultless, self-gratifying greed. I couldn't be judged and I didn't care if I was. If it was broken, I fixed it. If it needed money, I found it. I had an answer and a solution for everything. That is, until that same summer afternoon in Boulder when an unexpected phone call interrupted my mountain reverie and I learned that baby Kennedy was about to be born. That day I learned unequivocally that the time for taking my life for granted was over. I rushed to the hospital as fast as I could but the baby came early. He didn't cry.

Yes, the illusions had ended and a new awareness about life began with the birth of our fair-haired, blue-eyed child born with Down syndrome. He was the first challenge I couldn't fix, buy my way out of, walk away from, or change. In the face of all the questions I couldn't answer, I decided instead to celebrate our infant son. I soon came to learn that Kennedy was in fact the ultimate gift, the godsend, and the more-than-worthy partner who would finally make me into a man. Unbeknownst to me, that man would shape himself into a warrior dedicated to protecting a child who might never be able to protect himself. And as it came to pass, our baby Kennedy came for all the rest, for all the other Kennedys just like him. Thanks to him, a crusade for the defense of thousands had begun.

When committing oneself to
transforming the world, remember
every change begins within.

Chapter Fourteen

The Courage of One: Lorraine Espinoza

"The greatest happiness of life is the conviction that we are loved—loved for ourselves, or rather, loved in spite of ourselves."

—*Victor Hugo, poet and novelist*

One of the most unforgettable people who has come into my life thanks to Kennedy is an arc Thrift employee named Lorraine Espinoza. She's been employed by the company since 2006. Among other things, she's a gifted poet. Lorraine embodies everything arc Thrift stands for—a life with purpose, fulfillment, and belonging. Her success is everyone's success. Her deepest thoughts, shared with anyone who cares to read them, are preserved in writing, thanks to a family member who inscribes her work for her. Her poetry says it all, like this example:

The Fish
The fish looks like a shark.
It's very big with many teeth.
It moves quickly through the water,
    swimming fast and straight,
    never missing a turn. It's not very scary.

It just looks like it needs somebody
  to help it smile.
If it smiles, that will change the day
  into a very happy one.
Maybe it needs to hear a few funny jokes...

From "The Fish" by Lorraine E.

Unbidden, a new poem forms in her mind, and does so often. Like so many others, it bubbles to the surface and sets her free. She can hardly wait to get home where someone will write it down for her. Meanwhile, she sits by the entry to a store, in her wheelchair, and often, a large, folded blanket covering her lap and legs. You can't see it, but she holds her heart in her hand.

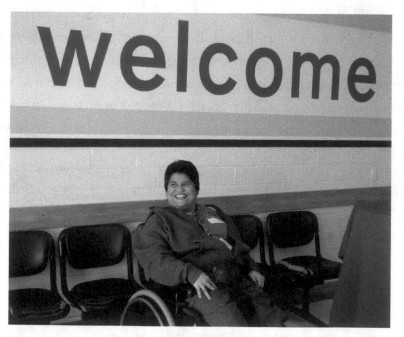

Lorraine Espinoza

Lori, as she likes to be called, greets you with the biggest smile imaginable and huge brown eyes, often accentuated by pale blue, luminous eye shadow. Her body arches as she expresses her happiness at your arrival. (Unruffled by the spasm, she assumes it doesn't bother you. It does not bother her.)

"Welcome to arc Thrift," she says, her head thrown back, eyes facing upward. Her arms shake slightly, fingers spread, showing off neon-pink, polished nails. When her back relaxes and she's looking at you directly again, she shares the warmest expression on the planet. Her face captivates you with round cheeks, full lips, and straight white teeth. She seems ageless, but you guess she might be in her mid-thirties at most. A chic, mod haircut shows off sunny highlights over dark roots.

"Welcome," she says again. "We're glad you're here."

*****

Lori is one of several employees at the largest arc Thrift store in Lakewood, located on the far west side of the city in a huge retail strip center. She lives with her parents, now in their seventies, and gets to work each day by taking Accessoride, a special bus service created for individuals with disabilities. Her manager likes to call her a greeter, but I would say she's much more than that. She's humanity personified, positively glowing. In winter months, you might find her in a bright, puffy, zippered jacket; in summer, in a colorful blouse. She is each and every one of us if fate had looked another way. You can barely pass her without acknowledgment, her presence so strong, her magnetism so real.

Lori is unable to walk, or even adjust her posture. Occasionally she slips deeper than is comfortable, and then asks for assistance to raise her in her chair. This involves lifting a portion of her fully grown body, and adjusting straps that fasten her into her new position. Similarly, when eating, she requires great assistance, often in the form of being fed with a napkin placed firmly around her neck to prevent food from spilling onto her clothing. When bowling, which is something she loves to do, she requires a bowling ramp upon which the ball is placed by someone assisting her. Then someone helps with her hand using a finger or two to push the ball just enough to go down the ramp and into the lane.

That said, Lori's warm welcome simply changes the space you're in—in fact, the very reason you might have come in to the store. What from the outside appears to be a big box, fluorescent-lit, retail space suddenly feels like home. Racks of clothing disappear before your eyes, aisles of bric-a-brac shrink away. Lori's eyes hold you fast.

Customers easily draw near. She captivates them with her essence. She is an unexpected welcome to the casual shopper, and like the aforementioned fish in her poem, not scary at all. No matter her difference or her wheelchair. She's there to help. People stop, approach, and extend their hand.

"What's your name?" they ask, their mission temporarily forgotten.

*****

Regardless of age, education, gender, or financial privilege, cerebral palsy (CP) impacts the physical body, and for some, the mind as well. Coordination is sometimes out of control, muscles are sometimes rendered useless. With CP, even the very breath that the rest of us take for granted at times forces the spoken word to be expressed in uneven bursts. But those who have CP can choose whether or not to be its victim. They can fight back, with the right help, and hold on to who they really are. If they're lucky, they can have a life full of reward, based on their ability. And if they're very, very lucky and live in Colorado, they might also be employed by arc Thrift where persons with all kinds of physical and intellectual disabilities are welcome, not just those with cerebral palsy.

Lori had a job before this one. She worked in a small company trying to do tedious piece work. She lacked human contact, and her work lacked significance or personal meaning. But today, after having served at several other arc Thrift locations, she's recognized and adored by many. Not only by fellow employees, but by regular shoppers, too, who count on seeing her and hearing her familiar voice. She feels connected, wanted, appreciated, and part of a team.

Despite her physical challenges and limitations, Lori's enthusiasm is contagious. Her ability to laugh at herself and others is beyond endearing. She makes friends quickly and evokes interest, not sympathy. In fact, she inspires profound respect. Not long ago, at one of my CEO group meetings, Lori informed my fellow colleagues that she was gunning for my job because she "would throw better parties." And when I chided her at bowling night about this boast, she responded she "was throwing me under the short bus." She dares quip with the best of us.

Behind this terrific sense of humor and good will is a sensitive person profoundly aware of herself and others. "I really like my work," she affirmed. "I love it here. One day, however, I would like to work with children, reading stories or giving out toys. What I love most though, is to write. (That is, I dictate, and someone else writes for me.) I started writing when I was around ten years old and now I have over 250 written pieces. I dream of having a book of my poems published someday. I don't know how or where, but that's my goal.

In the meantime, working for arc Thrift has made me want to make things better for people who have CP like me."

Most of all, Lori is proud to be who she is. She's outspoken, unafraid, and confident. One year, the local fire department sent a calendar to all the arc Thrift stores featuring the various firemen as part of a fundraiser. Lori looked it over. She fell head-over-heels immediately for Mr. October and let him know as much. She is all-woman. Sometimes when people use wheelchairs, we forget how much they are like us.

Lori's affections run deep—for her parents, for her store manager Scott, for her colleagues, and especially for one of the store cashiers, Seth. She also says she loves me (those are her words) and she has written one of the most beautiful notes of appreciation I have ever received.

When customers head for the exit doors, arms full of bargains, they shouldn't be surprised to hear a cheerful voice call out, "Thank you for coming to arc Thrift today to do your shopping. Thank you, most of all, for helping people like me."

Here's another poem:

I Love You Just Because
I love you just because you
    support me.
I love you because you make me
    feel like a queen.
You make me feel like time stops
    and I am the only one who matters.
You hang onto to every word I say;
    like I am saying words you've
    never heard before…

Even if I don't always have you, I
    will always remember who you are.
I will remember, I got my
    confidence from you.
You're not my mom or my dad,
but you still mean a lot to me.

From "I Love You Just Because," Lorraine Espinoza

*****

Lori's poetry has even inspired me. In fact, her poetry inspires me so much that one Christmas I decided to gift her with a poem in return. I'd like to share it with you:

When you enter a room,
    you light up everyone around you.
Your smile, and the way you laugh
    and make people feel is a special
    talent.
You make people forget their
    problems and their struggles,
    and you make people believe in
    themselves.
You find a way to appreciate
    everyone and let them know you
    appreciate them.
Life is more fun when you're
    around; you help us all focus on
    what's important;

helping others and making a
  difference in their lives.
You glide in and out of rooms in
  your wheelchair, making others
  respect you,
envious of the ease by which you
  move.
Your poetry inspires us, it makes
  us better people. You smile, your
  laughter, and your humor inspire
  us too.
When you greet people, you are
  the best and friendliest greeter
  anywhere. People mistakenly
  think you have a disability. You
  don't. You have an ability to lift
  people's spirits and allow them to
  lead greater lives. And we thank
  you.

**The muse does not judge. She
comes to all of us, ready to fill our
hearts with words and song.**

Chapter Fifteen

A Man Named Robbie Hall

*"We are made strong by the difficulties we face,
not by those we run from."*

—*Unknown*

Robbie Hall

Naturally, several others among our persons with disabilities use wheelchairs. Each one is directed toward jobs that are suitable for his or her kind of mobility. A wheelchair rarely holds anyone back.

Besides, all of our entrances, restrooms, and employee lounges are wheelchair accessible. We don't have to worry about any of them. We have others with different kinds of mobility issues, but they persevere regardless.

One of my favorite, most courageous individuals ever to work at arc Thrift was Robbie Hall. In his mid-thirties, Robbie stooped when he walked due to congenital abnormalities that required more surgeries than he could specifically recall. The bold structure of his face, out of alignment under a shock of brown, unkempt hair, was nonetheless compelling, even attractive in a way. A series of surgeries from mild operations to open heart, covered a broad range of issues, comprising a great deal of risk and recovery time.

When I first met Robbie, he was unsure of himself and spoke haltingly, possibly more out of fear then shyness. I could only imagine how he might have been treated on the playground at school or among his more able-bodied peers. I learned that he loved teddy bears growing up and continued to as an adult; his room at his group home was filled with them, all of which he had named and who were his "friends." He told me once he had long and deep "conversations" with them.

As I got to know Robbie better, he eventually broke out of his shell to the point of becoming quite the social butterfly. He would approach me at social and work functions, and it would soon become difficult to get a word in edgewise. Robbie became quite conversational, and spoke about his activities and plans with enthusiasm. Anytime he was in my car for a ride to an event, we'd have deep conversations about life. He made me laugh many times with his insight and annoyance of people not doing things the way he liked, especially at work where he was very particular.

Over time, Robbie became one of our most valued and appreciated employees, famous for teamwork and assisting gratefully in almost any task presented to him, even beyond his role of performing janitorial tasks in one of our stores. He participated in a social group comprised of our employees with disabilities, attending events with us, including trips to the movies, zoo, dinner excursions, and more. He also took part in the learning program we created for our employees with disabilities, and took great pride in his accomplishments in a series of classes covering a wide variety of practical learning experiences. Occasionally, up until his untimely and unexpected end, he presented in front of our management group, talking about his host home where he lived with providers who gave him shelter and love. He spoke about his job, dreams, goals, and more.

Robbie was both sensitive and kind. In conversation with him, one quickly forgot his "disability" and appreciated the beauty of his connectedness. For the unappreciative, his appearance may have startled. But for his friends and those who knew him, his true beauty quickly emerged and inspired others. We thought so much of Robbie that we made him one of our Heroes of the Year at our annual gala in 2013. We present these prestigious awards at formal ceremonies to honor employees who conduct themselves with distinction, and who make tremendous contributions to our company. Robbie was deservedly proud.

This past spring of 2017, Robbie underwent unexpected surgery for a brain tumor, a difficult and worrisome situation for him and all of us here at arc Thrift. Fortunately, the operation was reported as a success and, soon after, he was recovering at a rehabilitation center in nearby Broomfield, Colorado. He started talking and was beginning to resume his former self.

In his own words, as spoken during one of our manager's meetings and video recorded, this is what Robbie said about his life:

"I was a duck. Really, that's what people said. My back curved so sharply I walked bent over and kind of sideways. Kids laughed. Some quacked. Some said I was retarded. Not even my mother could protect me. I hated going places in public or being with other children because people stared. They jeered. My childhood was very difficult due to these kinds of incidents. "Looking back, I'm not sure how I lived through it. All I wanted back then was to escape my own body, but I couldn't. Night after night, year after year, I dreamed of standing straight and sitting upright, just like everyone else. I dreamed of being normal. I dreamed of being free.

I can honestly say that my life began when I discovered arc Thrift in Denver, because they welcome people like me. They help us find work that we can do easily. Most of the people employed by Arc are different in some way; I'm one of many who confront some major challenge every single day. For some it's physical, for others it's intellectual.

"The good news is we don't have to do it alone. The employers at arc don't judge. Instead, they accept. None of us has to worry about what others think. I've learned that my disability doesn't have to stop me from having a sense of independence, from earning a living and making friends. I have a life I love and can dream about the future. No, I don't look like anybody else. But it doesn't matter to me. I'd like to meet you."

*****

Following the aforementioned surgery, Wanda, the manager at the store where Robbie worked, sent us an email. In her short message, she quoted Robbie who, grateful for all the cards and letters that poured in, repeatedly said, "If it wasn't for arc Thrift, where would I be?"

All I could think of in response to her message was—*If it weren't for Robbie and all our special employees, where would arc be?*

As I approached writing the final draft of this book, we learned that Robbie's overall prognosis was not good. Things had taken a turn for the worse, and his time was clearly limited. The news was a setback. Each and every one of us who had seen Robbie rise to the greatest heights imaginable considering his disabilities, felt more than defeated. We sadly contemplated his loss; he was one of us, a shining star. For any employer who has ever encouraged close-knit workers, you can understand our collective pain. Mine was immeasurable, and I resisted thinking of his end. Our remarkable Robbie would be sorely missed.

Our company is a family.
A family mourns its own.

Chapter Sixteen

Claire

"Being deeply loved by someone gives you strength, while loving someone deeply gives you courage."

—Lao Tzu, Chinese philosopher

Kennedy's mom gave birth to another child, our son Aidan, a few years before we were finally separated. Kennedy now had a younger brother. I discovered later that raising two boys as a single parent over a period of several years wasn't easy, especially while working full time. My ex and I shared our lives with them, on a fully half-time basis. Kennedy and Aidan grew close, always together at every occasion. They shared the same room, school, social events, and holidays, and enjoyed playing, roughhousing, and watching TV together. Unlike my other kids, they fought very little. When it was my turn to take over and spend time with them, I relied on good friends and even my office staff at arc Thrift headquarters to help out with driving and other errands. It took creative scheduling and planning, patience, and flexibility. In retrospect, it seemed like I was always in the car, always heading somewhere. It was exhausting.

On a personal level, I knew something in my life was definitely missing. Following my divorce, I wasn't happy. About the split, I had no regrets; I couldn't go on the way things were in my former relationship. The separation was inevitable, and for so many reasons, maybe even predictable. Nonetheless, life was incomplete. I knew I needed a partner who could go the distance, celebrate life's joys with me, and deal with its sorrows. I needed a wife to be by my side.

*****

The boys initially attended school in Lafayette, north of Denver, where Kennedy's mom still lives. When Aidan was but eighteen months old, he had been diagnosed with some kind of sensory processing issues that later began to affect his ability to learn. I was concerned to learn that he was falling behind and thought he might need more help. I wanted closer supervision of them both.

I had the boys with me five days on and then five days off, commuting to Lafayette on many days to get them to school. It was demanding, even grueling for me and especially the kids, but we all did what we had to do to make it work. I often had to rely on after-school care during my watch.

Aidan and Kennedy stayed in that school in Lafayette up until Kennedy's fifth grade when we decided to put them in the school system in my neighborhood on the southeast side of town. They both needed special programs for different reasons. Aidan, now behind almost two years, actually caught up in less than 24 months because of the change to a much better school, Belleview Elementary in the Cherry Creek School district. He later switched to Campus Middle School in 2016. Both boys are now at Campus Middle School and doing well, but the successful transition took some tutoring and our family taking a very active role in their school work.

Around the same time, another momentous change in my life occurred, a turning point that, for me, just keeps unfolding.

As a mid-fifties bachelor, following the separation, I began dating. My friends were ever on the lookout for the right girl for me. It became more and more clear that I not only needed a woman to help me raise a family, but to share my dreams and goals as well. That was a big priority; besides having someone to love, I needed a partner who could help me realize my vision with arc Thrift.

The children from my first marriage and the daughter from my second were growing up fast, already in high school or college by then. The real need for stability and happiness was for my two younger boys, caught in the midst of my shifting emotional and professional life. Still, I wanted them to have a real family in a real home, with a wife and mother who cared for and cherished them.

No one I'd met seemed right, and I wasn't ready to rush into anything. I was extremely wary. My previous marriages had ended for various reasons, and I began to wonder if I had ever understood who I needed or why, or how to stay committed. Perhaps, when I was younger, I'd confused my priorities. I couldn't let that happen again. I kept looking.

After numerous introductions via friends and acquaintances, I finally met Claire, someone I now believe I'd been looking for all my life. I'd been separated from Kennedy's mother by then for five long years. Claire was everything I'd hoped for and more. Beautiful, smart, and a widow with three boys of her own, she had a refined confidence and a warm personality. Fit and petite, she looked like a knockout in everything she wore. Her spring-green eyes reflected a world of hope, and her bright smile lit up a room like sunshine. Claire didn't doubt any of my dreams and seemed to understand completely what I wanted to do. The attraction between us was immediate. We had chemistry.

Claire had lost her husband to a rare disease; he succumbed far too young, in his mid-fifties. Self-reliant, she had been a teacher at an elementary school level and understood kids. Like me, she too was searching to belong to a family again, to be part of something solid and real, with someone she loved and who loved her back. I was ready to fulfill that role.

Our romance was intense; I fell head over heels, and felt sure that this woman could go the distance with me, and with Aidan and Kennedy too. What she didn't know about individuals with special needs she said she would learn. I found a kind of connection I'd never experienced before, plus a feeling of intense appreciation and gratitude. Maybe that's what happens when you learn to love someone so entirely. Perhaps my experience with Kennedy had opened my heart to a deeper level and given me new eyes to see value and beauty, and appreciate it in new ways. Claire had it all. I wanted her in my life forever.

I laughed when she told me her friends thought she was crazy to buy in to all that came with my proposal—ex-wives, children of various ages, a son with a disability, a passion for all persons with disabilities, and a relentless drive to succeed, no matter what. But she understood the challenges before her, and in spite of the enormity of entering into my complicated, sometimes chaotic world, she said "yes!"

"I really wanted to love someone again," Claire told me. "I felt an emptiness in my life. Someone later asked me what I was looking for in a man, and I answered that I wanted to marry someone with compassion and humor, but most importantly, of moral integrity— someone respected by others for his work or life. Money or looks were not important."

Could I say that Claire was the woman who came for me at the perfect time? More than a partner, she was capable of helping me get wherever I needed to go. Then, as now, I had someone to rely on, lean on, and share my life with. I was ready for Claire Holz Lewis. Our marriage in the fall of 2014, attended by supportive family, colleagues at arc Thrift, and good friends on both sides, might just be the most wonderful day of my life. Except that each day with Claire gets better, so I can't be too sure.

Love encircles us like sunlight
and illuminates the way for
everything else to come.

Chapter Seventeen

Meet the Ambassadors

*"I do not care so much what I am to others
as I care what I am to myself."*

—*Michel de Montaigne, philosopher*

Imagine a glittering hotel ballroom with elegant tables set for a celebratory dinner. Hundreds of guests in party finery converse and mingle against the backdrop of live music. Every one of them is a friend of arc Thrift, looking forward to a remarkable evening about to unfold. For beyond the cocktails, the sumptuous meal, great music, and an exciting, fast-paced live auction, this night, like every annual gala since 2010, will honor three outstanding Ambassadors (arc Thrift employees to you) who deserve special recognition.

Up until now, you might have noticed that I've referred to our large staff of persons with disabilities as employees, but in truth, we like to call them "Ambassadors," carrying our message to our customers, their families and friends, and the greater public, whenever they are asked to speak. The idea for this special designation came from one of our own: David Eaton, who believed that he and his colleagues could do far more than just work for us. They could tell our story—and theirs—better than anyone else.

David Eaton

David is an African-American with a bright smile and generous personality. Born with cerebral palsy, he was put up for adoption by his birth parents, then offered again by his adoptive parents. Incredibly, he was adopted once more, and then given up again! After this disruptive and discouraging start to life, he spent the remaining years of his childhood with a series of less-than-caring foster parents.

Despite his relatively high intelligence, David was put in a special school for children with intellectual disabilities, burdened with low expectations and low educational standards. But David was resilient. On his own after high school graduation, he worked at a series of low paying, low-skilled jobs, without much recognition or sense of accomplishment. He came to our company as an assistant in our corporate office, performing various functions, such as shredding, copying, filing, etc. Then he had an idea. Why not form a group of employees with disabilities who could go out in public and speak about our company and mission? He wanted to call them "Ambassadors." They could talk about our mission and their experiences with our company.

Thanks to David, we started our Ambassadors group with ten employees, more than ten years ago. As indicated in the second chapter, we now have over 300 Ambassadors. An Ambassador speaks at each of our monthly managers' meetings about his or her job, friends, dreams, families, and what it's like to have a disability, as well as how people with disabilities should be treated. They often do radio and TV interviews for us, and make presentations to community and business groups.

I was asked recently if I was ever nervous when an Ambassador stepped up to the microphone. Since I had gotten to know David Eaton extremely well, I never doubted from the first his ability to communicate with a crowd. He had a lot to contribute, and never even needed a rehearsal. What I discovered that morning, to be applied from then on, was merely a need for me to prompt the speakers with great questions: the responses were always heartfelt, spontaneous, honest, and often humorous. That seems to be the best way to conduct these occasions with all our Ambassadors, and audiences are always moved.

One of my favorite stories about David took place in our break room a few years ago when he was eating Mexican food. "These chili peppers are so hot," said David, "that if I put a couple of chili peppers in my pocket, I think I could leap out of my wheelchair and walk!" What David didn't know was that his creativity and idea for the Ambassadors' group would leap out into our company and create a lasting legacy. After all, as unique as they are, the Ambassadors all share the fact that they have their own challenges and their very own compelling stories.

Then, as now, candidates who applied to work at arc Thrift and become our Ambassadors have come to us from every corner of life, referred by friends or families, teachers and therapists, but mostly by word of mouth. In truth, we always try to carefully consider hiring a referral. Once our new candidates are interviewed, we try to find the perfect jobs for them— everything from soliciting to accepting donations, to sorting, or hanging clothing items. Some prefer to stock shelves or do janitorial work. Others help keep the front of the stores neat and clean, including the dressing rooms. Other candidates excel at customer service, cashiering, or serving as greeters. Some enjoy bagging, accounting, or serving as receptionists. We match jobs to people, with their interest and skills, and sometimes, even create new jobs that did not previously exist.

This is why, on the night of the annual gala, we invite families, sponsors, teachers, therapists, and anyone in touch with the broader arc Thrift community to raise a toast, not only to our generous benefactors and supporters, but to our large family of Ambassadors and the three select honorees among them who are named arc Heroes of the Year. These special heroes are nominated by managers based on their contributions each year. I humbly make the final decision.

Shown here is a group shot at one of our many informal gatherings. Note Arcky, our feathered mascot, the bluebird of happiness, in the background. He is our friendly logo. The "V" is for victory, and yes, everyone is smiling.

Ambassadors at the 10th Anniversary gathering.

Anyone can have a dream
and make it come true.

Chapter Eighteen

Party Like You Mean It

The Galas and Why They're So Important

"We make a living by what we get,
but we make a life by what we give."

—*Winston Churchill, British Prime Minister*

Our 2016 gala, a sumptuous dinner with our popular arc Thrift fashion show, is one recent example of a very successful fundraiser. That event attracted a record-breaking 600 persons in attendance, an exceptional evening all the way around.

Former Aurora Police Chief Terry Jones, well-known from his help in handling the infamous 2012 Aurora movie theater shooting, recruited colleagues from several departments in the metro area. His recruits took part in "Heroes Among Us," the theme of the event, and served as escorts in the fashion show, an annual highlight set to music.

Jones, who chaired the event with his wife Lori, assembled a crew that included Aurora Fire Department Deputy Chief Cindy Anderson, retired Deputy Chief Dan Martinelli, Aurora Police Commander Ernie Ortiz, and Arapahoe County Sheriff Dave Walcher. These peace officers accompanied nine arc Ambassadors who were chosen to model.

In the professionally orchestrated fashion show, each Ambassador was beautifully attired in outfits selected by image consultant Patti Shyne, who selected clothing from the racks of arc Thrift Stores. Among the models were Neveah and Rudy Sutorius, the niece and nephew of Terry and Lori Jones. Nevaeh has Down syndrome and Rudy is on the autism spectrum.

"Without the support of arc Thrift," said Lori, beaming at her family members, "they wouldn't be where they are today."

To give you an understanding of the caliber of the three individuals honored that night, it's important to get better acquainted with the 2016 arc Heroes of the Year: Kingahnah Grant, Elizabeth "Beth" Burczyk, and Joaquin Rondo.

Kingahnah Grant graduated in 2012 from Overland High School in Aurora. He worked for a short time at arc Thrift doing warehouse work and answering phones before coming to the southeast Centennial store to be both a greeter and a runner. He enjoys coming to work, seeing his friends, and helping customers. He loves music—especially pop—and dreams of one day being a D.J. Because he is something of a pop culture enthusiast, he is also planning to start a video blog that will address current issues and the local music scene. He says he wants to offer his many fans his particular spin on all things "trending."Kingahnah enjoys writing poetry and stories and playing video games as well.

Elizabeth Burczyk graduated from Golden High School. In 2012 she earned two certificates in drama from Red Rocks Community College, where she studied stage hand and costume basics. As a serious actress, her favorite character played so far is the Wicked Witch of the West in a production of *The Wizard of Oz*. A lover of travel and foreign cultures, Elizabeth has been to South Africa, Zimbabwe, and Botswana, where she viewed numerous wild animals at game parks. A gifted speaker, Elizabeth proudly presented a workshop at the National Down Syndrome Congress Convention about the art of stage makeup. She also sits on the board of the Rocky Mountain Down Syndrome Association as a Self-Advocate. Elizabeth was a model in a recent Global Down Syndrome Foundation's "Be Beautiful Be Yourself" Fashion Show and at last year's "Born to Be Me Gala" presented by arc Thrift. She was also that year's valedictorian from arc University. A dynamo of boundless energy and endless ambition, Elizabeth hopes to rent her own apartment some day and help other people with disabilities. These days, she works as a department assistant and cashier at our west side Green Mountain arc Thrift store.

Joaquin Rondo's life story seems almost miraculous. He weighed only two pounds when he was born three months early on November 6, 1984, and remained hospitalized for 45 days. But he was a fighter, even then. According to his caregivers, when he came home from the hospital, he was still so small he slept in a sheepskin-lined shoebox.

Joaquin grew into a fine young man and has worked for the arc Thrift Stores for six years. He started as a volunteer until he was hired, and now works in production, sorting shoes; he is also a department assistant at the Austin Bluffs store in Colorado Springs. Joaquin loves to play video games and watch *Godzilla* films over and over again, all 28 of them. He takes Kung Fu lessons and has achieved an orange belt in ancient oriental weaponry. He loves going out with his friends to the movies and dinner. More recently, he has started experimenting with drones. At home, where he lives with his mother, he owns a cockatiel and three dogs. Joaquin's goals in life are to live independently and travel the world.

*****

Proceeds from monies raised by the gala event help fund programs and services that arc Thrift supports and provides for the many Coloradans with intellectual and developmental disabilities. In addition to individual ticket holders who fill the room, we are always indebted to the many community leaders who donate to our cause. Among our many loyal supporters at this event were old friends Michelle Sie Whitten, executive director of the Global Down Syndrome Foundation, as well as Craig Fleishman, a prominent Denver attorney, and Terry Vitale, a very successful Colorado magazine publisher and society favorite. The list of ardent supporters and donors to our cause is too long to list here, but we couldn't be who we are without them.

Special supporters, always in attendance are Colorado's former First Lady, Frances Owens, and her daughter, Monica Owens Beauprez, who never miss a year. At one time, Frances Owens actually worked for us as our official Community Relations director.

"I accepted the position at arc Thrift because I had an affinity for people with disabilities," explained Frances. "The one thing I've learned since my tenure there is that working with the Ambassadors has taught me that no matter what the disability, they only want what everyone wants: friendship, acceptance, appreciation, and stability. The many host homes and caregivers who provide them with daily care and services become their support system, giving them the opportunity to thrive and to be productive."

Frances really couldn't have said it better. Giving anyone a reason to get up in the morning and go to work in an environment where they are appreciated, respected, and rewarded, might just be the most significant thing any employer can do.

Having the Ambassadors in my life makes my own life more worthwhile; it justifies the time and effort I invest in this company, head, heart and soul. It's simple. The more I give, the more I get in return. This is a formula few can achieve, and most of us wish for. But it's not something that only I own. You can experience it, too. I wish you could see and feel this reality. It is life changing. I wish you could join me here for just one day.

*****

In 2017, we experienced another record gala, this time titled Celebration of the Human Spirit. We hosted well over 600 attendees this time, totaling income of over $300,000 gross and $200,000 net. Lovely anchorwoman Anne Trujillo from KMGH-TV Channel 7 added some celebrity glam as did Murphy Houston from KOSI 101.1 radio. Retired Director of Marketing and Public Relations for Volunteers of America Colorado, Jim White, along with Vice President Carrie Benz of Denver's Janus Henderson Investors, emceed the event. Spirits were high and our supermodel Ambassadors that night had an absolute ball.

Adam Horney, son of Karel Horney who established Adam's Camp, an alternative camp experience for children with disabilities, actually tried to kiss the blond policewoman who was his escort (to the audience's delight) and Dustin Schrage, Sarah McHenry, and Nick Daniels sashayed down the runway with style and swag. The Ambassador Heroes of the Year this time were Heather Pyle, Tara Wehry, and Katherine Moore.

Heather Pyle is a greeter at the Westminster store and also an enthusiastic participant in Magic Moments Theater of Denver. (Magic Moments Inc. promotes the arts by fostering an environment of acceptance, growth, learning, and support for participants and the larger community by inviting people of all ages, with or without disabilities, amateur or professional, to perform in original musical theater productions.) She is an outstanding public speaker who loves to talk to our customers.

2017 Gala
From left to right: Model/Ambassador Sara McHenry, Ambassador Aaron Walbert, behind him are Models/Ambassadors Dustin Schrage and Shanna Gunnink. Anchorwoman Anne Trujillo applauds.

Tara Wehry works as a processor at our arc South Broadway store, where she sorts clothes and sets out merchandise. The store is both a refuge and a place of employment for her, since she has survived an extremely hard life, filled with bullying. She loves reading romance novels and coming to work every day.

2017 Gala
Heather Pyle with Denver
Mayor Michael Hancock.

Aaron Walbert
with Anne Trujillo.

Katherine Moore, from Littleton, Colorado, works in the Littleton South Bowles location. She loves coming to work to what she calls her arc family and is passionate about sports, and loves to play football and go camping with her family.

It's important to understand who our honorees are because it's helpful to see how much they are like the rest of us. They have their talents, their dreams, and their aspirations. We shone the spotlight on them that night with the help of a beautiful video produced by Channel 7 (KUSA-TV) for us, thrilled that those attending were able to learn more about them. The video made them larger than life.

Following a lively auction and spectacular cash donations, Denver Mayor Michael Hancock graciously joined us and took photos with our heroes. I had the pleasure of reminding everyone that the next gala in 2018 would be our 50th anniversary as a company, truly a mega-event not to be missed.

Together—family, friends, employees, and supporters are raising an entire community of persons who can celebrate life.

Chapter Nineteen

The Joy of Learning

arc University

"The mind is not a vessel to be filled, but a fire to be kindled."

—*Plutarch, Greek essayist*

How do you help a person move forward in the world?

Offer them the knowledge they need to grow, think, and create, for one thing—even to master basic life skills. And beyond that, offer them whatever else their minds thirst for.

In 2013, in conjunction with a prominent foundation in Denver, we at arc Thrift created arc University for our employees with disabilities. To operate this university, with its citywide campus, we drew upon volunteers from the greater Denver community to teach 90-minute classes on a variety of subjects, including handling money, operating computers, cooking, pet care, fire safety, sign language, online safety, doctor visits, wood working (boat and birdhouse building,) personal hygiene, and more. Classes were held wherever we found a host location. The idea was to keep our students motivated with stimulating and fun opportunities for learning.

To help us qualify for an annual operating grant from one of our foundation supporters, each of our students take pre-and-post tests to measure how much they have learned. Results are impressive. The annual program consists of twelve monthly classes followed by a commencement ceremony, replete with certificates and "degrees." In an arc University curriculum, it's important to note that the classes are always modified so the student can easily access the information.

One might well ask how you modify learning for persons who have IQs of 20 to 70? It's not easy, but it can be done. Content is focused and often condensed. Learning is always fun. In some cases, individuals choose to repeat the classes while others breeze right through. We do whatever it takes.

Our staff designed the program so if an Ambassador participates at all, they receive a basic certificate of completion. All that is required is attendance and participation, and the criteria does not measure pass/fail or correspond to a typical grading system. It merely acknowledges attendance. If the participant enrolls in six of the twelve classes, they receive a "bachelor's degree"; participation in nine of the twelve is rewarded with a "master's degree," and participation in all twelve classes is rewarded with a "PhD."

The annual afternoon graduation program—a fun, raucous, and joyful affair—is always held in a spacious venue to accommodate the hundreds who attend. Friends, family, and students enjoy a catered reception beforehand. Excitement fills the air as diploma recipients take their seats in wide rows, easily accessible by those using wheelchairs. Smiling "students" most often seen in work aprons and jeans behind counters and in the stockrooms at arc Thrift Stores, on this day glow with pride, many dressed in suits and ties or colorful dresses and high heels. Others sport their flashiest sneakers and bright T-shirts, whatever they feel most themselves in, everyone looking their very best. Most notable is how they assist each other. Those who need a shoulder to lean on or a wheelchair pushed forward don't have to look far.

For arc University's fifth graduation ceremony in 2017, we awarded thirty master's degrees, thirty PhDs, ten PhDs "emeritus" (for their second PhD), and five "distinguished" PhDs emeritus (for their third PhD). As smiling recipients walked across the stage during the graduation ceremony in front of a cheering audience, one might have thought it was a Harvard commencement, given the pride and joy exhibited. Wild whistles, whoops, and hollers are standard.

Keep in mind that all of our graduates have varying degrees of intellectual or developmental disabilities. Some retain a fair amount of learning, some a little, and some retain nothing at all. Some of our students aren't even verbal.

No matter. We designed this program to be as much for fun and enjoyment as for learning, given that most of our graduates have had very poor experiences in school. Class attendance and this kind of recognition gives them a feeling of self-confidence and pride many have never experienced before. Receiving the achievement certificate is an epic event, experienced with deep appreciation and even a kind of awe.

Bird houses, left to right: Rico Torres, Ryan Maly, Michelle Knight.

Elizabeth Burczyk builds a birdhouse.

Sailing at Chatfield Reservoir.
Beth Goymerac, Kathy
Thurlow, Erin Curry

As we all know, traditional learning styles can be programmatic and rigid. What we have learned here at arc Thrift is that learning can happen anywhere, anytime, for anyone. Learning actually awakens a hunger for more learning. It's lifelong.

At the end of this event, I felt compelled to share my feelings with all in attendance. Each graduation is for me a reckoning of my own hopes and aspirations, and an affirmation that we are doing the right thing while building a solidly growing reality. In part, this is what I said at the 2017 graduation:

Congratulations graduates! You've done an amazing job earning your degrees and certificates, and we are all very proud of your hard work and commitment to earning your degrees, as well as the amazing jobs you do to help our company.

Graduation ceremonies are a time for joy.

I am honored to present the commencement speech tonight. I think of you as great people, employees, and great friends, so it is truly an honor. Commencement speeches are usually given by speakers who share experiences, values, and advice. I'll do my best to share some of mine with you.

I've had many experiences in my life. Successes and failures; great joy in love—and disappointment in love; finding myself—and losing myself; a great family, children, and a great wife; jobs I've not particularly liked, and jobs I've really liked. Many things I've done well, and some things I haven't done as well. The best times for me have been with my family and my children and working with people I really enjoy. Through all these experiences I've learned to appreciate the good things—family, job, and friends—the experiences that count.

Lloyd with Kinghanah Grant.

The values I've come to appreciate are many: working hard, making a difference, taking care of family, helping friends and people in need. We need to appreciate the simple things, like how to set goals, do everything in your power to help those you love most, including your friends and even people you don't know who might need your help. I believe we should try new things, not give up, and try to become better each day. We must learn to stand back up when we fall. My advice to you?

Be who you are. Live your dreams. Dream big. Fall in love. Love your families. Love yourself. Don't let anyone think you are less than who you are. Be proud of yourself. Be proud of your Arc degrees, and your jobs with Arc, and how much you help Arc and other people with disabilities. Know that you are our heroes. Know that we look up to you, enjoy being with you, and that you teach us more than we teach you. Above all, appreciate your friends. Treat everyone like you would be treated. Have fun with your hobbies—whatever they are. Have fun watching movies, dancing, singing, playing music, being creative, or cooking…whatever you choose.

When you look in the mirror, know that you are beautiful, both inside and out, and that everyone at Arc sees your beauty. And know that the work you do helps provide millions and millions of dollars for people all across Colorado with disabilities, helping them find jobs, places to live, get medical help when needed, and help in school.

Know that the work you do helps hundreds of nonprofits in Colorado and across the country fund the important work they do through our vehicle donation program—millions of dollars each year. That work provides money to Cerebral Palsy Colorado and helps provide thousands and thousands of vouchers to families in need. The work you do also helps us collect thousands of pounds of food each year to help people who are hungry. And the work you do helps provide jobs for all of your fellow Ambassadors. Remember you are an important person, a person we love, and you are making a very big difference in the lives of so many people. Above all, know you will always have a job at arc, and we count on you each and every day. We are proud of you for what you do at arc and at arc University. Congratulations to all of you for your hard-earned degrees!"

I'm not sure everyone there caught or understood every single word, but I hope they felt my appreciation and love for them all. As I read this address over again, I can tell you one thing: When I was a graduate, I wish someone had said all of this to me.

Time and money spent on education is never wasted. It's how we install value in living every day. Pride is the greatest gift of all.

Chapter Twenty

Kennedy Now

"A man never stands as tall as when he kneels to help a child."

—*Knights of Pythagoras quote*

Kennedy Lewis, Zach Holz, Aidan Lewis

It's Christmas morning and the house is abuzz with holiday commotion. Claire's high school and college-age sons sit in the family room watching TV; Kennedy and Aidan are sampling cookies in the kitchen. The air is filled with the tantalizing scent of roast brisket and potatoes, and the spicy fragrance of homemade apple cobbler.

In the living room, the floor beneath the brightly lit Christmas tree is covered by dozens of wrapped packages in every size and shape. Against the window, behind the living room sofa, a branched menorah stands in silhouette against the warm morning sun. It's a reminder of the rich tradition Claire has brought into our family.

The boys can hardly wait. As the rest of us gather round, Kennedy and his younger brother tear into the stash of gifts with gusto. Even with all the excitement for this long-awaited morning, Kennedy sits back and enjoys watching his brother unwrap presents as much as he enjoys doing it himself. He waits patiently while they each take turns. One by one the treasures come forth: new posters for the boy's bedroom, Harry Potter memorabilia, a Star Wars T-shirt. They love it all.

When the stack is reduced to ribbons and paper and the pair are busy installing batteries in their remote-control flip cars, I marvel at my teenage child with Down syndrome whose laughter and happiness fill our house. Still struggling with verbal clarity, he chatters nonetheless, a running dialogue between Aidan, his stepmother, and me; his ready smile is the affirmation that everything in Kennedy's world is A-okay.

Life with Kennedy continues to be one of daily challenge and reward—mostly reward. Not too long ago, Claire took Kennedy to the Kent Denver Country Day School varsity basketball banquet. It was an end-of-season celebration for her teenage son Zach, plus the other players and their parents. The players would all be acknowledged during the night. Some of the parents stood up and spoke. Kennedy, apparently inspired by what was taking place, decided to give a speech, too. He stood up at the same time as another parent—the CEO of Western Union—was talking. Kennedy was unaware that he was interrupting. The gentleman decided to defer to Kennedy and sat down.

Full of unabashed confidence, Kennedy began his proclamation, the words tumbling out as fast as he could form them. He spoke about Claire, his brother Aidan, about basketball (illustrating the sport with a dribbling-like motion), about the concession stand, about his favorite candy, about soap, shampoo, and more—everything that mattered to him at the moment. He simply wanted to share. Needless to say, the crowd received him like a champ with a warm round of applause.

Naturally, I wasn't surprised when I heard about it.

That's my boy! Never hold back, a lesson I think many of us could benefit from. Kennedy's self-confidence shames me. Would that I had the same bravado.

Over the last few years, Kennedy has also become famous for giving "toasts" at our family dinners, which, regardless of the holiday or occasion, usually conclude with the word "cookies." (Why not? It's such a great thought to leave one's guests with for the evening!) By allowing Kennedy to join in and simply be himself, all of those who share these moments get a glimpse into his world. And it's a beautiful world indeed.

*****

When I was growing up, I can guarantee you that you never saw people with disabilities, not in schools, shopping malls, or at the movies. It's hard to imagine, but in my parents' generation, and even in the baby boomer generation I belong to as well, they were sent away to large institutions and families were told to forget about them. People were ashamed. It's absolutely heartbreaking to think about it. Our fast-growing, communicative, utterly delightful son reminds me every single day why I'm doing what I do and how important it really is.

Thanks to positive reinforcement, acceptance, and love, Kennedy clearly feels good about himself. He has no fear. During a recent interview with a local newspaper, Kennedy bounced into the living room and stole the attention of the reporter, interrupting the talk. As I often do, I turned to him and asked, "Kennedy, are you a good dancer?" to which he replied "yes!"

"Are you smart?" I asked? "Good looking?"

"Yes, yes, yes!" he confirmed, grinning and dancing across and out of the room. The intrusion was typical, done and over before it got started. He just needed my reassurance that he wasn't being left out, that he was there. No problem. He got the reassurance he needed. I believe it's important to give him positive reinforcement every chance I get, something we practice at work every single day with all our employees with special needs.

Now at age 14, Kennedy is popular at school and accepted by his peers. He currently reads at about a second-grade level, after having undergone extensive speech and occupational therapy. He lives each day at a time, without complaint. According to Crystal Minor, Kennedy's caseworker at Campus Middle School, Kennedy is well adjusted and thrives in his unique program there, mainstreaming some subjects such as social studies and science while attending special education classes for reading and math. He also chooses electives that have included robotics, theater arts, and art, a few of his favorites.

In the Cherry Creek School District, students with significant support needs are served through what is called the Integrated

Learning Center (ILC) programs and attend their neighborhood school as much as possible. Out of 42 elementary schools, 34 ILC programs have specialized staff; all middle schools and high schools have a severe needs (ILC) program. At the secondary level, inclusion focuses on electives, after-school activities, and the general school community. Core subjects are sometimes taught in the resource room and applied within the community as the students move into their high school and transition years. Community-based instruction is gradually increased during the student's secondary school years. In addition, Kennedy benefits from ARC educational advocacy where his teachers meet with us regularly to evaluate his progress. He also receives speech therapy there, a huge bonus.

Added Crystal, "Some content can be overwhelming for Kennedy, or any student with special needs, such as chemistry, for example. It's important to note that individuals with learning disabilities have uniquely different needs. Some might have an intellectual disability and something else as well, such as a speech impairment and/or autism. Mainstreaming these children was a groundbreaking move instituted not too many years ago. It's been so successful it's become a national trend. From my point of view, I'd love to see us all teaching this way every single day, everywhere."

Kennedy's response to the challenges at school is varied. Sometimes he's resistant and yet still does the work; other times he's more enthusiastic. But in essence, he's a happy kid, and, says Crystal, sometimes even a "goofball." He loves physical education classes especially because he's so very social. He also loves music and dancing, his favorite form of self-expression. Children at Campus Middle School earn free time, and when Kennedy has some, he chooses to watch Go Noodle on You Tube, an entertaining video with movement and songs. According to Crystal, he often seems to use music to get focused. (Go Noodle, with its fun, active videos, makes movement and mindfulness an integral part of the day, at school and at home, applicable to any field of study or recreation.)

My wife Claire occasionally substitute teaches at Campus Middle School. She had this to add:" I have observed Kennedy only once this year in class…for art, and noticed that he is well liked by many of the students. They love doing high-fives, connecting with big smiles. Kennedy will frequently put his arm around another student as he walks in the halls. He often holds the door open for a line of students in the morning as well."

All I know is my son gets up and gladly goes to school each day. His language skills are broadening and his speech improving. We are lucky to have him in such a wonderful environment.

*****

Children with Down syndrome, for the most part, have these amazing qualities—kindness and appreciation—that are as important as any other. They override any deficit. It's ironic, but I've seen with my own eyes that many professionals spend a lot of time trying to make people with disabilities a lot more like us. Why, I wonder? I am beginning to think there should be some kind of therapy to make us much more like them.

The Campus Middle School in Englewood, Colorado, is among hundreds of Colorado schools that take advantage of Arc's educational and advocacy programs every single day. As Kennedy matures and matriculates out of the public school system, he will actually qualify for Arc's employment and housing assistance, and could even be a self-advocate on Arc's legislative fronts. The school will also eventually help him with a transition program out of high school to make sure he's getting the right kinds of support. Adulthood, after all, presents a whole new set of challenges, but we'll be right behind him. I feel like the essential reinforcements are just over the hill.

*****

As I look around me, I recognize that life has a way of telling a person they're headed in the right direction, that the universe is in alignment. You can imagine how great I feel knowing that my eldest daughter, Hannah, who graduated *magna cum laude*, also spent time as a researcher at the famed Linda S. Crnic Institute for Down Syndrome at the University of Colorado Anschutz Medical Campus. Groundbreaking research is taking place there in so many areas, especially regarding Alzheimer's disease, currently a condition without prevention, treatment, or cure. Many believe a hidden clue lies in the Down syndrome population. Some doctors at the Colorado University Medical School at Anschutz, for example, refer to people with Down syndrome as "a medical gift to society." It turns out their unique biology makes them ideal for medical research in heart disease, immune systems disorders, soft tissues cancers, and of course, Alzheimer's. It's exciting to think that as she continues her studies in a PhD program, she will know more than I ever will.

A mere coincidence? Divine providence? I'll never know, but you can be sure that in our household, Kennedy has siblings who care and understand him and are just as committed as I am to making the world a better place for him and all the kids out there with special needs. Each of my five children and three stepchildren are unique in their own way. My greatest hope for all of them, but especially Kennedy, is that they stay as happy as they can be and fulfill their potential, whatever that is. I hope that Kennedy has solid relationships with the people he loves, and a pleasant and positive family life. In short, everything I ever wanted for myself I want for him. Nothing less. Whatever lies ahead for Kennedy is unknown, but this much I do know: He has made me a better person simply by being in my world. How can I ever thank him for that?

Proverb: The child is the father of the man. In my case, this has never been more true, any way you look at it.

Chapter Twenty-One

It Takes a Village

"We have all known the long loneliness and have learned that the only solution is love, and that love comes with community."

—Dorothy Day, journalist

Graduation Prom Party
Left to right: Rico Torres, store manager Scott Jeffers, Seth Weshnak, store manager Paul Trujillo, Robbie Hall.

To the hundreds of volunteers who help us put on our parties and graduation ceremonies and who help teach classes for our Ambassadors, and to the caregivers and parents who make sure our community of persons with disabilities gets to work every day and home again, and is nurtured with love, we are hugely indebted. These generous individuals come from every walk of life. They make arc Thrift possible. They are our everyday heroes.

Even though I am always thanking them, publicly or personally, it's also not unusual for some of them to thank me. As an example, I want to share a letter with you. It came from a person fulfilling a community service assignment as part of a judge's criminal sentence. Its message assures me we're on the right track.

"To whom (at arc Thrift) it may concern,

I just want to express my gratitude to you and your staff. Know how impressed I was as a volunteer recently at your store. Though my hours there were required for court purposes, not only were they painless due to the attitude of your staff, they were enjoyable. Rather than scathing judgment, meaningless tasks, and an unwelcome vibe (one that I have become accustomed to in dealing with the criminal justice system in nearly all facets), your staff shone; quite the opposite. They were friendly, polite helpful, offering guidance and support always. You truly serve the community and offer hope for social reform in numerous ways and are proof that what you do can work for all who are involved. Specifically Joe, Johnny, Julie, Nick, and Bill were individually wonderful to work with. Cathy, Ryan, and Leo couldn't have been more pleasant or friendly. Thank you sincerely and good luck to you all. I will spread the word about Arc and your stores. Keep doing what you are doing because you are doing it right and you do it well. Again, thanks again to your entire staff. God bless and Peace!

Sincerely, Thomas G.

Each time I read this note, I'm reminded that one simply never knows whose life we may touch and how. I am humbled by this kind of thanks.

*****

At the recent 5th Annual arc Graduation ceremony held at the Arvada Cultural Center for the Arts and Humanities in 2017, select awards were given out to special individuals, especially volunteers and staff members. One of them, the Rem-Arc-able Buddy Award, went to Melody Rutledge, an employee from our Austin Bluffs store in Colorado Springs. Melody's story, I'd like to think, is representative of many who work at arc Thrift and is part of what endears her to all of us. Here is how she told it:

"Eighteen years ago, I was shopping at arc and saw two Ambassadors in the store. (They weren't called that then, however.) I watched them work and was so impressed. *I'd like to work here,* I thought. I was hired soon after and found my place in the bric-a-brac, or home accessories, area.

"Every department has an Ambassador. Mine is Danny. He is in his twenties and has issues around anger and trust, but he loves working here. He takes time to test our toys, and capably packs up our holiday decorations after Christmas for storage until the next season. We have lots of interaction and laugh as we work.

"Long ago, before I came here, I'd be dishonest if I didn't admit that if I saw a disabled person, I was indifferent. Now, however, no matter who it is, I stop to talk. I've learned that they are people just like us. It's a 100 percent turn around in my appreciation and awareness.

"Once a month, Danny and I, and often a few other department heads and Ambassadors, drive up to the arc Thrift organized events in Denver, in order to attend classes or social outings. Rain or shine, snow or hail, we are there. It's just over a hundred miles each way. What's really amazing is that we all talk in the car, nonstop.

"'What are we going to do today?' one of the Ambassadors might ask.

"'What do you think Lloyd is going to wear?' someone else inevitably poses. (For some reason, this topic is always of great interest.)

"They are always impressed, as am I, that Lloyd knows them all; that he actually remembers each of their names. In fact, his energy and commitment are contagious. Over time, I have come to realize that there are people at this store who really need us; who really need *me*. We are part of their stability. The Ambassadors clearly become attached. I've learned for example, that when I am not there for some reason, Danny has trouble focusing.

"I know for certain that I am making a difference in somebody's life and I'm so glad. I want to work here until I have to retire."

*****

One of my favorite caregivers is Karen Gray, a host home provider, who, with her husband Keith, looked after Robbie Hall for more than 18 years. Karen is the person he lived with and loved during the time he worked for us. Without her, he might not have survived at all.

"Robbie taught me so much," said Karen. "Mainly about humility. And generosity. This man had a heart of gold. He was generous and giving. In spite of all his challenges, he craved independence. He took the bus every day to work even though people offered him a ride. When we traveled, he also traveled with us to places like Disneyland, Hawaii, and his absolute favorite, to the monster truck show in Las Vegas. He had a profound relationship with my husband who loved him like a son. Following his operation for a brain tumor and his rapid decline, we were grateful to arc Thrift enough for stepping in and helping out. At that very difficult time, Lloyd came over to see us personally to ask what he could do and provided us with services we needed at the time. We were so touched."

*****

Karen Gray was also with Robbie at the 2017 arc University graduation ceremony. At the time, Robbie was still in recovery from the surgery and in a wheelchair. As she guided him through the crowd, he was greeted right and left by all who knew him. Robbie shook hands and exchanged hugs; he had a special talent of making everyone feel valued and important.

My former assistant Kristie Gamboa Cheyne remembered the last few times she was able to visit with Robbie at rehab, at the graduation, and in his caregiver's home. Each time she went it was the same greeting. "How are you Robbie?" she'd ask, and he'd reply "Well, I'm still here."

As he was leaving the ceremony after receiving his diploma, she reached over and gave him a hug. He grabbed her hand and said, "Walk me out."

She walked beside his wheelchair and he held her hand all the way out to the parking lot. She finally said, "Robbie, I'm going to need my hand back," to which he replied, "Some people are just hard to let go of."

*****

That's how I feel about losing Robbie Hall; I'm still having a hard time letting go. It was only a short time later that he succumbed to his tumor. His death was mourned by all of us within the arc Thrift community, his personal family, his host family, and his church. His funeral brought out sympathizers from across Colorado. As an example of one of our best, Robbie was a dedicated participant in our arc University program, and over the course of five years, rarely missed a class, earning several degrees, including a "PhD." About a week before he passed, he asked to be the valedictorian for our 2018 graduation ceremony. I agreed, and now plan to declare him valedictorian in memoriam. Shortly before his death he told his caregivers how proud he was of this distinction.

Staff member Dominick Rivera remembered when Robbie attended a dance held for our Ambassadors in 2015. It was the very same day that Dominick's own father had passed away. "When I told him my father had passed," said Dominick, Robbie replied, "Don't worry. The angels will take care of him."

A beautiful thought. I'd like to believe they'll take care of Robbie too. For arc, Robbie's passing was a tremendous loss, and he is greatly missed. I always thought of him, not as someone with a disability, but as someone with extraordinary abilities to be kind, thoughtful, loving, and encouraging in the workplace and in his community.

I often think that society looks at the wrong people to be their heroes: athletes, celebrities, actors, etc. The real heroes are those with the greatest hearts. In this vein, Robbie Hall took the prize. He will be long remembered.

Greatness is never measured by wealth or fame, but by how we treat others.

Chapter Twenty-Two

Santas, Sweethearts, and Star Wars

"People rarely succeed unless they have fun in what they're doing."

—Unknown

Taylor Shelsta and "Santa".

Throughout the year, arc Thrift creates festive social occasions we can share with our Ambassadors, mostly daytime experiences that they can access easily. We arrange transportation, buy bulk tickets to films and help arrange coverage at the stores, thanks to our many volunteers. Some of the most memorable events in the past 48 months might be attending the debut of the *Star Wars* film release *Rogue One*, viewed together by some 200 members of our "family," all transported one way or another to the Belmar shopping center in Lakewood. (They had other film options as well if this was not to their liking.)

Dominick Rivera produces the much-anticipated Valentine's Day luncheon/social, held for the last four years, a group favorite. Either a live band or a DJ supplies the music, Valentine cards are sometimes exchanged, and dancing provides plenty of fun. For those who are shy, the staff urges individuals onto the floor, taking a hand or guiding a wheelchair. Everyone has a good time.

On fishing outings or trips to parks, Ambassadors use the buddy system, two individuals paired up for safety. Once a year in September they are hosted by the Colorado Parks and Wildlife department for a day of fishing with gear supplied by one of the local outdoor sport retailers. This is now one of our most popular events. (Luckily for the fish, it's only catch and release.)

Said Rivera about his role as event coordinator, "Four years ago, before I was hired for this job, I believed I had a lot of patience. Now I know the difference. I'm pleased to say that I now have far more understanding of people's abilities, and am more aware of my own strengths and weaknesses. I try to stay calm and collected no matter what. The main thing is—the Ambassadors are having fun. I am proud of what I do."

*****

Closest to my heart is our winter holiday celebration. The second week of December each year, hundreds of Ambassadors don their best to gather at the Link Recreation Center in Lakewood, Colorado, for a fun-packed holiday lunch. They come by bus, carpool, and family transportation. The giant recreation hall is abuzz with chatter, old friends reconnecting, and new team members finding their way to welcoming tables bright with holiday decor.

The attendees here, as always, are bound by their uniqueness; none of them perfect in our familiar use of the word, but challenged in some way by disabilities not always immediately seen. Yet words like beautiful and handsome still apply, and many more. These are the courageous, the undaunted and the hopeful. They burst with energy and share spontaneous giggles. They exude charm, curiosity, and a rare sense of connection to one another, even to strangers.

Some have facial features shaped by Down syndrome, others have arms and legs altered by MS or cerebral palsy. But all meet your gaze head on and offer a sincere smile. Most introduce themselves to visitors and special guests immediately, extending a hand. "Merry Christmas" they might say, grinning broadly. "I am so-and-so." For the most part, they're not shy.

The teasing and joking between ambassadors and managers runs non-stop. Couples form. Some hold hands. Everyone smiles. An outsider might wonder what in the world makes everyone so happy. What is the arc Thrift secret?

I believe it begins with the mere fact that they are here. It's about acceptance. They feel welcome, safe, secure, and not judged. Beyond that, it's important to remember that this community is very much like you and me.

arc Thrift Ambassadors at holiday party.
Former staff member Kristie Gamboa Cheyne and Alicia Adams.

They have feelings, not hidden deep inside, but right out front, their energy so palpable you feel embraced by their openness. These are real men and women, deeply aware of each other, and prone to the same chemistry the rest of us have. Some of them have sweethearts, some are even married. Some long for intimate connection.

On this day, they are celebrating the season together—a room of individuals with challenges who line up patiently, waiting to partake of a bountiful meal, and to swap the latest news from the various locations where they work. They reach out to one another with trust and affection. They wave at me and at one another across the tables with quips and jokes.

I put on a Santa suit, make a speech in honor of the occasion, and then visit all the attendees. One year, I recall that one young lady dared ask me shyly that "when I don my Santa suit, would I please keep my distance?"

Because even though she knew it was me, the costume scared her.

Now, that's honesty for you. (Frankly, I looked in the mirror before I took that costume off and I think I scared myself.)

Moving from table to table, I always want to be sure that everyone has a full plate and a gift bag filled with candy. Wherever I looked, I was met with smiling eyes that clearly said, "Thanks for inviting me. I'm glad to be here."

On this gathering, and every one like it, it's easy to confirm that arc Thrift is actually in the business of saving lives, maybe even saving humanity itself. We will not tolerate rejection of people with differences, but seek individual value instead.

I'll tell you what: If there is a secret, I'd like to think it might be this. Our company, arc Thrift exists in order to teach the rest of us how to open our eyes and our hearts. This Christmas party, held year after year, is fun and all-embracing in its simple message. "Joy to the World." The truth behind our shared joy is that everyone here is loved, and our holiday message is always the same; those with disabilities must be counted, cared for, and given a chance to succeed. With hundreds in attendance; employees with Down syndrome, cerebral palsy, autism, and more, the atmosphere couldn't be more inspiring and uplifting. And it lifts me and our company up every single time.

Do not judge. Do not assume. People with disabilities are perfect inside and out. They feel and fall in love just like you do.

Chapter Twenty-Three

We're Not the Only Ones

"It is time for parents to teach young people early on that in diversity there is beauty and there is strength."

—Maya Angelou, *poet*

Twelve years and counting. The company arc Thrift has blossomed in a way I never thought possible. All around me are signs that the impact of our work is being felt across the state; my calendar is filled with appearances for organizations seeking our advice, wanting to learn.

It's hard for me imagine that I'm now the one many turn to help answers questions about persons with disabilities It wasn't so long ago that I was the one with all the questions. One of the greatest affirmations of my growth in the larger, national community for persons with disabilities was the invitation to speak at the famed Booth College of Business at the University of Chicago in 2014.

Returning to my alma mater, a tremendous honor, confirmed that the College of Business believed my story had merit and that others could benefit from it. I deliberated long and hard as to exactly how to deliver my message. Rather than offering them a strict business model, I wrote a speech titled "What I've Learned," a summation of my personal experiences with my son and arc Thrift over the previous ten years. In some ways, that talk was the springboard for this book.

In that presentation, I stressed the fact that I am not the only one with a commitment to inclusion. Activity is growing all around the globe. I wanted everyone attending to remember, as they went forth in their own endeavors, that caring is the job and privilege of everyone. Every individual, no matter what.

I found reassuring evidence of the power of change in author Rabbi David Jaffe's recent award-winning book, *Changing the World from the Inside Out*. A man devoted to seeking social justice in the world, his conclusions have fueled my aspirations even more. He said, in part, "Social change is the effort to shape the ways we live, work and play together in institutions, communities and nations, to reflect the inherent value of all people and the truth of the deep connectedness of things. Just as we grow as individuals by noticing and owning our imperfections and making choices to align our behavior with our ideals, so too do institutions and societies grow when enough people notice and own the imperfections in the social arrangements, and then decide to challenge those imperfections and change these arrangements to align with values like fairness, dignity, and freedom."

I couldn't have said it better. It's an absolute maxim for change. I hope you'll read it again. In truth, many companies now include and employ people with disabilities, achieving as we do, similar benefits for their businesses and its team members. Walgreens is one such company. Not long ago, a senior director of distributions created a multimillion-dollar facility in Anderson, South Carolina with the goal of creating a workforce with half of the employees being individuals with disabilities. Utilizing technology and streamlining the distribution process, this goal was achieved. Even more remarkably, this facility became the most productive distribution facility among all twenty-two Walgreens distribution facilities across the country. As a result, the other distribution facilities now incorporate the same concept of employing people with disabilities, and achieved similar results in productivity increases as did the original facility. And before the senior director retired from Walgreens, a program was adopted di-recting that one out of ten new hires at Walgreens would be a person with a disability.

Safeway is another such company with a long history of employing people with intellectual and developmental disabilities. In 2007, the company was specifically recognized for hiring 520 new employees with various physical, sensory, and developmental disabilities through the Council of State Administrators of Vocational Rehabilitation, CSAVR's network of agencies in the U.S.

CSAVR is focused on maintaining and enhancing a strong, effective, and efficient national program of public vocational rehabilitation services to empower individuals with disabilities to achieve the employment, economic self-sufficiency, independence, inclusion, and integration into the community.

Said then Safeway chairman, president, and CEO Steve Burd, "These employees are among our most productive, and we intend to build on this important program as a way of raising awareness and supporting people with disabilities." The company, which has since merged into part of Albertsons Companies, continues this important practice today.

The Council also recognized Safeway for its history of hiring and retaining people with disabilities, and the company's proactive work in the community in sponsoring events that promote hiring and accessible customer service for people with disabilities. These varied individuals help with a variety of roles in Safeway stores in

Colorado and elsewhere, working at jobs like stocking, warehousing, checkout, bagging, helping customers to their car, and other duties.

In a company training video that was widely distributed, an instructor told the story of a customer-service training experience of thousands of its employees. After this training, a young employee with Down syndrome went home and pondered how he could increase his customer service skills. The idea he hit upon was to copy quotes on pieces of paper and put them in customer bags as they were checking out. A few months later, the store manager called the instructor to tell her that she would never believe the result of the young man's idea; long lines were formed by customers who wanted to go through his checkout line. Plus, customers returned to this store more frequently, sometimes making daily or multiple trips per week, just to get more of his quotes.

Safeway and Walgreens are just two examples of companies that set a goal to make a difference and continue to do so today. A number of other great employers in America are known for employing persons with disabilities, among them are Kroger, Home Depot, Target, McDonald's, Walmart, Lowes, Goodwill, Chick fil-A, Panera Bread, Ikea, Stop and Shop, Lifetime Fitness, Market Basket and Fazoli's, to name a few. Every one of them has taken a stand and can be counted on to make the world a better place. Think about it. Could your company name be added to this list?

On a local level here in Denver, I personally applaud the efforts of a new craft brewery startup in Denver called Brewability Lab, a classic beer brewing facility. They intend to become the first in the world to train and employ adults with developmental disabilities in the craft beer industry.

The training process at Brewability is specifically adjusted by using repetitive, color-coordinated training that relies on repetition and visual cues. It's important to note that their system is not only set up for our staff, but for customers who may or may not have disabilities as well. Head Brewer, Tanner Schneller recognizes that, so far, these employees have been consistent and reliable workers which counts a lot in making a consistent product. Owner Tiffany Fixter launched Brewability after working for years in special education and recognizing that there just weren't enough jobs for this population. She's now hoping to offer job opportunities for adults (21 and older) with autism or Down Syndrome. See www.brewabilitylab.com

For more select Colorado agencies dedicated to improving the lives of persons with disabilities through advocacy, research, and/or employment, I invite you to see the appendix at the end of this book. History, details, and contact information are included.

When you consider innovations like the aforementioned programs from giants such as Walgreens and Safeway, it's thrilling to recognize the shift. We're not alone. All I can say is my fears for Kennedy have been subdued. It's obvious the world really is changing for the good. I dare imagine that by the time Kennedy is an adult, the world I'm dreaming of will be more than ready.

*****

If you are reading this book outside the United States and wonder what other resources are available to you besides those in Colorado, you might want to consider the SHALVA National Center in Jerusalem, Israel. Shalva, the Israel Association for the Care and Inclusion of Persons with Disabilities, is dedicated to providing transformative care for individuals with disabilities, empowering their families and promoting social inclusion.

I served on a U.S. advisory board for this remarkable non-denominational facility and am proud to say that Shalva provides an all-encompassing range of services for over one thousand individuals from infancy to adulthood, entirely free of charge. Additionally, they support and enable families to raise their children with disabilities within the family framework. Through nearly three decades of award-winning programs, Shalva partners with government, academic and philanthropic institutions in advocacy efforts to create a more inclusive society.

Located in the heart of Jerusalem on a hillside with sweeping views, the brand-new Shalva National Center opens new doors for individuals with disabilities and their families, offering programs, services and facilities never before available in Israel. It stands as Israel's beacon of inclusion and has become an international leader of innovative programs and research.

Adjacent to the new Route 16 Highway, the National Center has been designated by the Jerusalem Municipality to be the welcoming face of Israel's capital. The 220,000-square-foot campus is brimming with cutting-edge educational, therapeutic, recreational and vocational facilities. Six acres of inclusion parks are open to the public allowing children of all abilities to play and grow together.

Each of Shalva's programs are respectively recipients of the Israeli government's Ministry of Social Affairs and Social Services, Ministry of Education, and Ministry of Health's highly regarded recognition. It was my distinct pleasure to welcome the American Friends of Shalva to our home and share their story with dozens of caring friends and families.

Would it be fair to say that other parts of the world are ahead of us in raising the awareness level of the wider community? Maybe not. But it's encouraging to know that halfway around the world, in the heart of the Middle East, there's hope and encouragement for individuals and families in need. We only have to follow their lead.

I believe it's the dawn of a new era.
Compassion will take us into the future.

Chapter Twenty-Four

The Big Question

"Far and away the best prize that life has to offer is the chance to work hard at work worth doing."

—Theodore Roosevelt, president

I am often asked by my peers, other community leaders, and business CEOs, "How did I do it? How did I turn this amazing dream into reality? How did I create a mega-retail business that thrives the way ours does?"

Instead of all the various the answers I've given in the past, I wish I could have just handed them this book. In the future, I know I will. Because it attempts to answer that question throughout these pages, and much, much more.

In addition, one might also ask how I manage not only our retail sales 24/7, but also the massive export program we conduct, selling unsold product that we compact and bundle to well-paying customers overseas. On an average year, we easily send thousands of tons of used clothing to be recycled. It's an important revenue stream and helps us with necessary turnover, allowing us to also move new product into place and keep the stores looking fresh.

Imagine this: On a daily basis, we receive and sort thousands of donations by category, and fill our overflowing stores with new

Kinghanah Grant at arc Centennial store.

inventory, at the same time restocking and redecorating each store as needed to reflect the changing seasons and holidays. We process clothes, shoes, books, CDs, household items, linens, art, toys, jewelry, furniture, tools, and more. The totality is staggering. But we've learned how to handle it. It's more than a business, it's more like a marathon.

I could try to answer that initial business question in more detail, or just tell you how it definitely appears we'll be wrapping up 2017 with another record year—eleven out of twelve record years! And we'll do it in the face of adverse headwinds including online competition, traditional retail competition, the uneven weather, the economy, and the unfortunate closure of at least five other thrift competitors in Colorado. Proudly, I could also tell you how, with the opening of three new stores this coming year, and two additional stores next year, I intend to keep on track for increasing revenue, earnings and the all-important funding of the Arc statewide and the other programs we support. I could go on at length for pages about what we've accomplished, but I won't. Allow me to quote an esteemed advisor to our company, Frank Zaveral, recently consulted for this story, instead.

A longtime supporter of the organization in many ways, Frank has been with arc Thrift for over 15 years. As chair of the arc Thrift audit committee, his perspective confirms a great deal.

"I've seen the company grow in several ways," said Zaveral. "In part, in the number of stores. But more importantly, in the quantity of sales, not only from new stores, but from older ones, too. Therefore, our distribution to the advocacy statewide have increased, enabling them to hire additional staff.

Growth in the number of employees is stellar; over 1700 to date, with over 300 employees with intellectual disabilities. Once, I went out to visit some stores, and a young man, a new employee, was hanging clothes. When I spoke to him back then, he was nervous and shy. Today he is a beloved and productive worker there, and comfortable in his position. I attribute this to Lloyd's leadership and the emphasis he has on inclusion.

In truth, this concept was not understood before Lloyd's arrival. In the previous era, we had an unhappy environment. People felt threatened on many levels. We had a constant shift of emphasis, most of which didn't work. Lloyd decided instead to focus on one thing; our mission, and succeeded by making as much money for arc Thrift as possible.

When I asked him recently if he would like to be fifty years-old again, he answered, "Not really." He admitted how much he has grown and changed; factors that add up to being a very different version of himself.

The future of this company, I believe, depends in part on the future of the thrift business. Lloyd has been, and is still, working hard to create sustainability. He wants to be sure that the mission will be fulfilled. In my opinion, our real strength comes from our management group, reinforcing the mission ideal. Lloyd has the ability to teach them how to be problem solvers. Yet another plus is Lloyd's ability to make arc Thrift known in the community.

In the beginning, no one knew what arc Thrift was, who we were. He took it upon himself to get the word out and let people know. Then he inherited the idea of the annual dinner, which morphed into the annual gala, always focusing on the people, the recipients whom we have helped. The idea for a recognizable logo was also his idea, and thanks to a creative branding team, "Arcky', the happy bluebird, was created about eight years ago. Over time, Lloyd instituted an internal audit. And then there's his emphasis on store appearance, with items separated by size, and racks always kept full. In short, our CEO looks at every function in our business with a checklist, always working behind the scenes, making sure we appear organized, crisp and efficient. The result, I think, speaks for itself."

*****

Frank gives me a great deal of credit. Too much. In truth, we all deserve it, not myself alone. But I think you get the picture. I'm sure you do.

And it won't help you to understand further how I run my business. It's enough that you know how to run yours. By now, it's my hope that, thanks to this history however, you can begin to see what's missing in your business plan, or how you might add another layer to your own operation. More important, how you might broaden your thinking, open your heart, and think inclusively about hiring individuals with challenges and allowing them to share their talents with you. Think about it. Put yourself in this picture.

What I most want to do at this point is share my gratitude and thanks to my exceptional staff at arc Thrift headquarters; the engine behind this massive locomotive, ever-moving forward. First of all, to our wonderful senior leadership team, district managers, store managers and their team members. Approximately fifty staff mem-bers work at our west Denver office, from department directors, to marketing and public relations specialists, accountants, security/ loss prevention experts, Human Resources, IT techs, and all of our won-derful support departments. They're a most incredible team. They deserve recognition too.

In addition, a great many hardworking individuals man our ware-house in our maintenance and facilities department. And of course, there's the trucking staff, too. All these people, too many to name here, are all my team players, keeping us in motion day after day, year after year. My gratitude to them is not enough. And of course- our Ambassadors. Once again, without them we wouldn't be arc Thrift.

*****

Before saying goodbye, I'd like to tell you about one of the speakers who addressed the audience at our 2017 arc Thrift fundraiser —Faye Tate, the mother of one our very special Ambassadors, Elleana Elizabeth Wilson Tate. At the time of her presentation, Faye worked at CH2M, a world engineering giant whose own mission, "dedicated to laying the foundation for human progress by turning challenge into opportunity," sounds remarkably like our own. Her eloquent message to our attendees that very special night perhaps best puts into words the essential meaning of arc Thrift.

When Faye took the microphone, we were graced by a loving parent who wanted to share her deepest thoughts about her daughter's unique experience as one of our arc Thrift Ambassadors.

"Elleana Elizabeth has intellectual and developmental disabilities. And she is a proud member of the arc Thrift staff at the South Broadway store. She's been employed by arc Thrift ever since she was a student at the school for the deaf and blind in Colorado Springs.

Elleana was born premature; doctors believed she would only live seventy-two hours. Over time, backed by lots of prayers and tears, she grew stronger, so strong in fact she started to pull out the support tubes that helped her survive. Today, at twenty-eight, she is visually impaired, has learning disabilities, and walks with a limp, and yet she is a cre-ative artist, a member of Girl Scouts of America, is active in church and very social."

Faye continued. "They say it takes a village to raise a child, and I am so pleased to say that arc Thrift is part of that village. To me, you are like a family, one that cares for the people they serve. This company is not only a haven, but offers unique opportunities for many to become active participants of their community while learning how to enhance skills and build self-confidence. I want to thank arc Thrift from the bottom of my heart for all they do to enhance the lives of those with 'different' abilities. By providing support, you are helping to inspire young people like my daughter."

*****

Elleana Elizabeth Tate

In our eyes, dear Elleana Elizabeth Wilson Tate is more than special. She has a unique presence about her, a serenity and a positivity that others feel. She has a beautiful smile; an asset for her job as a greeter at the Broadway store. People are enchanted by it. She has attracted quite a following.

When Faye was done speaking, everyone in the ballroom applauded a mother's courage, and that of her daughter as well; two individuals who persevered where others might have quit. A standing ovation brought tears and cheers to some 600 believers who recognized the power of an organization to accept, protect, empower and embrace.

As I mentioned earlier, this year, 2018, will be arc's 50th year in Colorado, and we'll all be standing together again come September at the downtown Denver Hyatt Convention Center, celebrating like never before exactly who we are, what we stand for, who we serve, and the value and contribution of people with intellectual and developmental disabilities in Colorado.

Trust me, we can hardly wait.

Stand with us. Watch us soar.

Chapter Twenty-Five

My Challenge to You

"We are here on earth to do good unto others. What the others are here for, I have no idea."

—*W.H. Auden, poet*

It's a Monday morning in September, 2017 and the scent of fall fills the air with a bracing sweetness. The boys are back in school. Claire hurries them along as she makes an early breakfast and readies them for the short drive over to the school campus. As mentioned earlier, she actually has a part-time teaching position there, which created a huge opportunity to be in touch with the program, the boys' teachers, and their progress in general.

I can hear Kennedy humming the tune to one of his favorite songs while he dresses. Truly, music to my ears. He's happy about the long, hot summer being over and being back in school. He likes learning with his friends. I'm happy that he's happy.

I ready myself for another long day that involves travel, meetings, budgetary review, a warehouse visit, and a midday board meeting. Typical, really. But more important, I've been thinking about you—how I want to say goodbye, and what exactly I want to leave you with.

I feel compelled to say this: If you're one of those readers who likes to open up a book and read the last chapter first, and you're reading this right now, I hope you won't continue. Stop. Stop and go back to the beginning and start over. Take the time to step into my world and start at page one.

But if you have read the contents and we are almost at the end of this story together, I hope you enjoyed a peek into my remarkable world. Realize that I have only highlighted a handful of the outstanding people who make arc Thrift what it is. I wish you could meet them all.

For the sake of understanding the purpose of this book, I'd like to summarize much of what you have read the same way I did when I spoke at the Booth School of Business in Chicago a few years ago. There, I tried to tell this entire story and introduce the audience to all its endearing characters in a thirty-minute talk titled "Nine Things I Know Now." I covered a lot of ground—as much as I could, given the time.

I'd like to think you got the better deal. All the details.

There's no need to repeat the stories; I'd like merely to leave you with the lessons. These lessons apply to all of us, and it's my hope they might become part of your next step, your personal change, and your contribution to a world that's clearly changing for the better.

That world will hopefully be a place where diversity inclusion encompasses the intellectually and physically challenged, too. Those of us involved know it's an unending battle. I ask you to please join me on the battlefield and help turn the tide.

Here's what I know now and what I ask you to remember:

(1) Ducks Have Feelings Too and Are Beautiful in Their Own Way.
Robbie Hall taught us that the imperfect have their own beauty, measurable from the inside out. Never, ever judge a person by appearances.

**(2) Grace and Purpose Come Accidentally, and
Challenge Us to Respond.**

Achieving a state of grace arrives through action
and reflection. Understanding our purpose in
this world is a gift, often a long time in the
making. When either or both occur, rise up
to the shift and be grateful. When Kennedy
came into my life, he gave me the opportunity
to change. Be open to new ideas. When you're
given a chance to change, honor the opportunity.

(3) Everyone Can Be Inspired. Everyone.

No matter what you do for a living, seek higher
ground. Strive to grow. Find spiritual reward in
what you do; make your goal larger than it is
now. I found meaning and redemption in the
thrift industry and helping the community of
persons with disabilities. I challenge you to find
it in yours.

**(4) There's Music Everywhere, Even in a Blender
or a Garage Door Opening.**

Kennedy taught me that each of us marches to
a different drummer. It took a boy born with
Down syndrome to teach me to see and hear
clearly again, and to see beyond the challenges
to what really matters.

**(5) The Invisible World Is Visible If You Are Open
to It.**

Realize that society shuns the imperfect and

seeks to hide or cover what doesn't fit. Lorraine taught us that often fish with big teeth don't bite. Look past the differences. See with your heart. Maybe someone just needs a good joke that day.

(6) Poetry Can Be Found in a Smile or in a Laugh. Never underestimate the talents and skills of a person with disabilities. Art dwells within us; poetry is everywhere.

(7) Learning Can Happen Anywhere, Anytime. arc University proves that higher education is available to anyone, regardless of IQ. Everyone loves to learn. Everyone grows from it. Everyone should be eligible for this life-changing necessity.

(8) Caring Is the Job and Privilege of Everyone. Corporate culture is changing across the country, and around the world, as more and more employers see the benefits of hiring people with disabilities. But to affect society, no one entity can do this alone. We all have to join together.

(9) Imagination Is the Key to Life. Even the most disadvantaged among us can give birth to a brilliant idea. Listen, validate, and consider. David Eaton, the creator of the Ambassadors, taught us that by honoring each other, we might light up the world.

I hope these simple truths resonate deeply and are truths you, too, can use. I feel certain that, as time goes on, I'll be adding to that list. I hope you'll join me in making one of your own, a list with one goal—to enlarge your vision, uplift your impact wherever you go, and become a change maker.

To reference author Rabbi David Jaffe one more time in *Changing the World from the Inside Out*, I ask you to savor this:

"As change makers, our deepest yearnings for justice, peace, and wholeness are generally less about helping others and more about creating something together that is central to our own identity. Knowing clearly what motivates us to act is what makes things real. When we are intimately familiar with our deep yearning, our involvement takes on a different quality than when we simply know intellectually that something is a good idea. When we have clarity about what drives us, we are present, and *this* makes all the difference."

Be present and be true to yourself. Listen to your own heart. Do the right thing. Support those with special needs and include them in your world. That's what I ask. And as a closing note, I ask you to consider one more thing: Do try to see things as they are, not as they appear.

In an airbrushed, photoshopped version of reality, individuals we encounter in magazines, on film, and on television often seem too beautiful to be believed. Sadly, that's the version of life most of us see every day, whether we like it or not. We know it's not real. It's fake. We've been duped. But we buy in, regardless.

Thanks to this ongoing charade, our culture has presented us with an impossible standard few can ever measure up to. Even produce in our grocery stores must be without a blemish to be sold, and each and every day, perfectly edible food is thrown away. It's a waste and a shame.

Lloyd and Kennedy at home.

Let us not perpetuate that world. Let's see life as it really is, and people all around us for who they really are. See them from the inside out. I have re-imagined a perfect world and it's filled with humanity of every kind. As a parent and a business leader, I am grateful for what I've learned. Sometimes people just come out differently. That's all there is to it. It's time to acknowledge this diversity and celebrate life. All of it. In the words of the impactful leader Martin Luther King, Jr.: "So often we overlook the worth and significance of those who are not in professional jobs, in the so-called big jobs. Whenever you are engaged in work that serves humanity, for the building of humanity, it has dignity and it has worth."

May your work help build a better
world, and may the light of awareness,
knowledge, and compassion light
your entire life as it has lit mine.

APPENDIX

OTHER COLORADO AGENCIES MAKING A DIFFERENCE

Global Down Syndrome Foundation
www.globaldownsyndrome.org

Earlier in this story I introduced you to Michelle Sie Whitten, another parent of a child born with Down syndrome who embarked on this journey of discovery, education, and advocacy almost 15 years ago. Her personal commitment turned to the area of research and education, and thanks to her heroic efforts and the support of her parents, Anna and John Sie and the Anna and John J. Sie Foundation, the Global Down Syndrome Foundation (Global) was created in 2009—a non-profit organization dedicated to significantly improving the lives of people with Down syndrome through research, medical care, education and advocacy.

Michelle's first daughter was born with Down syndrome. At the time, the family personally experienced many disturbing situations around her diagnosis, healthcare and education—a familiar and sad reality. Prenatally, they were given incorrect information about the lifespan her daughter would have, and genetic counseling was focused on termination, not on educated choices.

When Michelle's parents first heard the news that their granddaughter would have Down syndrome, it was a kind of revelation. Their first reaction was, "We are going to love and nurture this baby no matter what! Of course, we were shocked at first, but it was as if the diagnosis itself instantly made us better people," says Anna, who earlier emigrated from Italy in the '50s with her father and brothers, settling in New Jersey. She knew something about feeling different and being accepted.

"Because of our granddaughter, we have a passion to help all people with Down syndrome," she continued. "This has become our life's mission. We want the best for her, but just as passionately, we want the best for all people with Down syndrome, young and old. As my husband says, from the cradle to the grave."

As a result, the Sies and their daughter vowed to change the bigger picture, not only in America, but worldwide, intending to educate governments, educational organizations, and society in general in order to affect legislative and social change so that every person with Down syndrome has an equitable chance at a satisfying life.

Relentless in changing the experience that they went through for countless others, Michelle has championed the cause of individuals born with Down syndrome all over the world.

Global's primary focus is to support the Linda Crnic Institute for Down Syndrome at the Anschutz Medical Campus, the first academic home in the United States committed solely to research and medical care benefiting people with Down Syndrome.  (Yes, this is the same Linda Crnic written about earlier in this book; the brilliant University of Colorado professor of pediatrics and psychiatry who dedicated her life to the unwavering mission of helping people with Down syndrome through scientific research.)

The Crnic Institute was the first in the United States to identify basic clinical and developmental research, alongside medical care for people with Down syndrome, as its core focus. The mission of the

Crnic Institute is to eradicate the medical and cognitive ill effects associated with the genetic disorder. Key partners of the Crnic Institute are the University of Colorado Denver School of Medicine, the University of Colorado Boulder, and Children's Hospital Colorado.

Since Down syndrome is one of the least-funded genetic condition in the United States, fundraising and government advocacy to correct the alarming disparity of national funding for people with Down syndrome is a major goal. The Crnic Institute provides the world's first fully integrated institute for Down syndrome with the highest quality basic, translational and clinical research, clinical trials, therapeutic development, medical care, education and advocacy in the pursuit of the mission.

Professionals at the Crnic Institute dare to embark down new paths, and have the courage to think about new ideas and measure new outcomes. They work to inspire others to join a global movement for people with Down syndrome.

Another integral part of the Crnic Institute is the Anna and John J. Sie Center for Down Syndrome at Children's Hospital Colorado. Anna knew research would take time, and while she whole-

heartedly supported the long-term efforts, she wanted more immediate help. She was concerned that most doctors knew little about Down syndrome, and wanted children with the condition to receive the best care from physicians and staff focused on the syndrome as soon as possible. She wanted accurate and unbiased information provided to women with a prenatal diagnosis of Down syndrome. And she wanted programs –lots of them.

"Why was it so hard to find a good music class, dance class, sports team or anything else for our children?" she asked. "Good teachers and good coaches can and do teach to all abilities. The issues I was hearing from other parents and grandparents didn't make sense to me. I wanted to turn everything upside down. I wanted the families of children with Down syndrome to decide what program would be so privileged to have their child – not what 'Down kid' was lucky to get into some program."

Anna's staunch beliefs led to the creation of the "Dare To" camps and the Be Beautiful Be Yourself dance classes aligned with broad-based community partners such as the Denver Bronco Cheerleaders and Football players, the Colorado Rapids, Regis University, Colorado Ballet, University of Colorado Boulder BUFFs, and many more.

*****

As mentioned earlier, funding for research for people with Down syndrome is a huge priority. It's shocking to realize that the National Institute of health budget in 2017 was $33.1 billion and only 0.0008 went to research for people with Down syndrome.

"Even within the developmental disability category on our side, we are by far the least-funded," says John.

"Fundraising and advocacy is a big part of what the Global Down Syndrome Foundation" added Anna. "Of course, I don't think any of us are really comfortable asking people for donations. But raising critical funds is the only way to truly create a brighter future for our children with Down syndrome. Every time John and I make that phone call for a donation, I think about those low expectations I grew up with, then think to myself 'not on my watch' and I make the call."

Global's marquee annual fundraiser, the Be Beautiful Be Yourself Fashion Show, is the single largest fundraiser for Down syndrome in the world. It brings nationally known Hollywood and sports celebrities together with the models and self-advocates who happen to have Down syndrome to raise awareness and funding to a sold-out crowd of nearly 1400 attendees. To learn more, please reach out to: info@globaldownsyndrome.org, 3300 East First Ave. Suite 390, Denver, CO, 80206, Phone: 303-321-6277.

Atlantis Community, Inc.
www.atlantiscommunity.org

Atlantis Community, Inc., is an organization that provides services to empower people with disabilities to integrate with full and equal rights, choice, and self-determination into all parts of society. That means employment, transportation, recreation, communication, education, access to public places, and affordable, accessible, and integrated housing.

Atlantis Community supports the right of people with disabilities to control their lives by providing a variety of consumer-driven services—from advocacy to education to transitioning people out of nursing homes and into their own apartments. It's a nonprofit agency run by staff, both with and without disabilities, that addresses the pressing needs of independence. Atlantis Community services the people with disabilities regardless of type or severity, through advocacy, benefits assistance (including Social Security, SNAP, Medicare, Medicaid), and housing referrals. They also offer assistance with housing applications and other resources, including transition support, peer counseling, women's and men's support groups, financial management (addressing payeeship, budgeting, etc.), and life skills activities and training. Atlantis Community, Inc., is an essential resource for so many in need.

The Atlantis Foundation, an offshoot of the former, has launched its newest effort, the creation of The Atlantis Apartments, which marks the dawn of a new era in housing for people in the disability community. It hopes to provide 60 accessible and affordable units with 25 percent of them reserved exclusively for persons with disabilities. They intend to support cross-disability accessibility to house people with intellectual and developmental disabilities, psychiatric disabilities, physical disabilities, traumatic brain injuries, and sensory impairments, and create true inclusivity within a mixed community, including varied income, family size, and abilities. As a member of the Atlantis Foundation board, I feel encouraged to see this kind of initiative.

Located in Denver's historic centrally located Baker Neighborhood, the forthcoming Atlantis Apartments will be an innovative, mixed-use facility with bus access at the site, nearby Light Rail service, and extensive retail, grocery, restaurants, and neighborhood-based shops nearby. The apartments will incorporate Universal Design principles to ensure that the built environment supports users with a wide array of abilities. The project will also incorporate technology, sensory elements, and way-finding cues to address multiple disabilities.

A utopian idea, its implementation raises the bar for those in need. Hopefully, it will become a model nationwide.

Tall Tales Ranch
www.talltalesranch.com

Pat and Susan Mooney of Centennial, Colorado, were inspired to create Tall Tales Ranch in honor of their adult son, Ross, who lives in

Colorado. Ross wasn't born with a disability; he suffered an acquired brain injury. He was a typical child who had lots of friends, loved to play sports, and dreamed of being a police officer when he grew up. At the age of 14, after undergoing a profound personality change, he was diagnosed with an aggressive genetic disease that deteriorates the white matter in the brain and eventually leads to death.

Following a bone marrow transplant in 2008, progression of the disease halted. Ross recovered and now lives with his injury, requiring a higher level of support. His parents wanted for him what every parent wants: a safe, supportive, and wonderful place to live where he might be able to experience community, responsibility, challenge, fulfillment, and acceptance.

The vision of Tall Tales Ranch, conceived as a "life sharing community," will be a place where adults with special needs can live and thrive, but also open to people who are not living with disabilities. The residents, called the Ranch Hands, would be committed to service, and to supporting our Ranchers in reaching their full potential. The goal is to encourage reciprocal relationships in a unique setting—one that will create a culture for those seeking a fulfilling life.

The mission of Tall Tales Ranch is to provide a supportive environment based on the beliefs that (1) all people deserve the opportunity to live and work in an atmosphere that honors their individual strengths and interests, (2) people learn invaluable life lessons by interacting with others who may not be like them, (3) all parents deserve to know that their adult children living with disabilities are safe, happy, challenged, and well cared for, and (4) all people deserve to be empowered to live a life that is respectful, purposeful, and dignified.

The envisioned Ranch would have horses and other small farm animals that ranchers can care for and the community can enjoy.

Ranchers will also manage community gardens and weekly farmers' markets.

Schweiger Ranch, a beautiful, historic property located in Lone Tree at I-25 and Ridgegate, south of the city, has donated a parcel of land to Tall Tales Ranch. This central location will allow easy access to the Ridgegate community (library, recreation center, restaurants, and local businesses). The accessible Light Rail line will give residents access to Downtown Denver and even Denver International Airport, helping to support and encourage their independence.

Founder Susan Mooney adds, "The thing that's really great is that more and more options are popping up, new alternatives, often led by parents. There's a lot of positivity, people working together."

Mooney believes that people living with intellectual/developmental disabilities deserve the same opportunities as everyone else. They deserve to work and play in the areas that both interest them and honor who they are as unique, valuable people, in a place that is cooperative, safe, and imaginative. They deserve a place where they can experience the friendship and community that makes life a fantastic story. In her words, "a place where they can live happily ever after."

Adam's Camp
www.adamscamp.org

The mission of Adam's Camp, now located in four states, (CO, AK, NH, TX and Ireland) is to realize the potential and develop the strengths of children and young adults by bringing together individuals and families with professionals and volunteers to collaboratively provide customized, intensive therapy, family support, and recreation in a camp environment. Adam's Camp envisions a world where children and young adults with special needs and their families are empowered with the courage, hope, skills and tools for a lifelong journey of realizing potentials and developing strengths.

Adam's Camp is actually a group of non-profit organizations, each providing a variety of intensive, personalized, and integrated therapeutic programs for children with special needs and their families as well as recreational programs providing fun, social connections and growth in independence for youth and young adults with special needs. They are successful because they meet the needs of the individual and the family in a camp setting, where healing and hope are contagious. The impact of their programs is clear: children with developmental delays experience significant developmental gains and have higher quality therapy experiences following camp as a result of the roadmap developed while there.

Siblings gain new strategies for living with a sibling with special needs while appreciating a quality camp experience themselves and parents gain new strategies to support their child's development, build a network of resources, and feel renewed from the respite they experience at camp. When a family member has special needs, the entire family has special needs.

Note: arc Thrift Ambassador Adam Horney was the inspiration for Adam's Camp in Colorado, based at Snow Mountain Ranch in beautiful Granby, Colorado. Adam's mother Karel was the founder of Adam's Camp. In turn, Karel was Adam's inspiration in becoming the strong advocate he is today

Adam has been involved with Developmental Pathways since he was a teenager. Aside from his involvement as a board member, he also enjoys attending social events held by Developmental Pathways and Continuum of Colorado, a local PASA. Adam is currently employed by arc Thrift in the Customer Service Department. He has an incredible work ethic, particularly made known after being recognized as "Employee of the Month." In his free time, Adam is a dedicated volunteer for the Denver Police Department, and is a tutor for Whiz Kidz through Colorado Community Church. He also enjoys spending time with his family.

For more information about arc Thrift Stores go to:
www.arcthrift.com

Happiness Surrounds Us

As a parting gift to you we offer the words to a rap song inspired by arc Thrift Stores.

"Happiness Surrounds Us" was written by Lloyd Lewis's stepson, Zach Holz and composed by Jack Friedman. You can hear it yourself at iTunes Music. http://ow.ly/yZeK30inOcG #arcthrift #thrift or go to https://www.youtube.com/watch?v=pPpiIN5wzSo&feature=youtu.be.

Walk into the room, put a smile on your face.
Grin so wide you lighten up the whole workplace!
All the insults and slander have no base.
We're all the same, have so much to showcase
and it's a safe space at the arc Thrift Store,
the kind of energy you just can't ignore.
Step through the door and you'll see at first glance
the employees beamin' cause they've been given
  a chance
to show what they can do,
all that they've been through,
all the false conclusions that have been unknowingly
  jumped to
lets them see things from a new point of view,
undo the prejudice and reveal what's true.
You're shopping at a place where
everybody can share the fact of knowing
no matter who you are, you belong there
and we got treasure to spare, so come and stop by,
the environment you see is the apple of your eye
cause at arc you'll never see anybody mistreated
  or conceded
over weaknesses. Kindness is all you need and

you're greeted with friendly faces, you can tell that
    they're thankful
we all have different strengths, just look from any angle,
the same old rigidness is what stops us from
    making progress
hatred of a human being is always hard to process,
brightens up your day to see everyone have
access to live a life they desire, you can see that we're
    all blessed.
Invest in people and you'll see they learn and grow;
accomplish the impossible, bigger then what you know,
goes to show you, never doubt what a person can do.
Everyone has obstacles that have been hard to
    go through
to make it through a problem, we have to do it together;
opinions, we all got 'em but know that nobody is lesser.
Walking down the aisle look at all the buried treasure;
is it items or employees, it's kinda' hard to measure.

Chorus:
Happiness surrounds us,
see the smile on our face,
everyone's accepted, your differences are embraced.
Come tell us your stories,
we all have ours;
there's no need for worry, just know that you're
    not alone.
Cause we're all special in our own way,
and nobody can go and rain on our parade.
We are different but spread the love
we show the world what arc's made of.

—Zach Holz, 2018

Lloyd Lewis:

Lloyd Lewis and his wife Claire live in Englewood, Colorado. In addition to being CEO of arc Thrift Stores and co-chair of the Colorado Cross Disability Coalition board of directors, Lloyd also serves as board chair for the Atlantis Community Foundation and Colorado Disability Partnership, as a board Vice Chair for Rocky Mountain Human Services, and is a past chair of the Rocky Mountain Down Syndrome Association. Lloyd holds a master's degree in business from the University of Chicago Booth School of Business, and prior to arc, held numerous roles in the private sector, including as a municipal investment banker for Smith Barney, a senior financial analyst for IBM, a director of finance for a publicly traded medical equipment company, and as a CFO for a high tech start-up company.

About the co-writer Corinne Joy Brown:
www.corinnebrown.com

An award-winning Colorado novelist with five books in print, a magazine editor, and a freelance writer for numerous magazines, Corinne is also a past-president of the Denver Woman's Press Club, and a charter member of Women Writing the West. She focuses on design, history, popular culture and personal transformation. She feels honored to have been selected to help write this book.

CPSIA information can be obtained
at www.ICGtesting.com
Printed in the USA
FFHW010157040319
50773836-56203FF